Lighthouse

K. L. Moore

ISBN:

979-8-9871601-8-3 (eBook)
979-8-9871601-9-0 (Paperback)

Chapter One - July

"Miss me already?"

Jordan Davis rolled her eyes with an affectionate smile at her best friend's teasing reference to the fact that they'd just seen each other at work. "I can only go a few hours without my Alex fix."

The sigh on the other end of the line stole away her humor. "Adam isn't home yet, is he?" She could tell that Alex was fighting to keep the accusation out of her tone, but it was enough to set her nerves on edge even more than they'd already been.

"He's been training someone new at the clinic. It's keeping him late while he gets her up to speed. Something about trying out a new program."

"*Her*?" Alex questioned, no longer masking anything. It was Jordan's turn to sigh.

"Yes, Alex. *Her*. Her name is Cassandra, got here a few months ago. She has been studying under him for a couple of weeks. They have to get her ready quickly, so he's been working long hours, that's all." The brunette pinched the bridge of her nose as a headache developed.

"Hey, don't get defensive. I'm your best friend, and I've known you the vast majority of our lives. When your husband spends long hours at work with a *female underling*, I have a right to be protective. Have you at least met her, considering how long she's been around?"

"I'm meeting her tomorrow. Everything is fine; he's been upfront with me about the situation from the start."

"I just don't want to see you get hurt here...be careful, please.

"He's my husband...I trust him." Jordan hesitated. "Hey, I've gotta go get some laundry done. I'll see you at work tomorrow, ok? Night, Alex." She hurried to hang up, anxiety churning in the pit of her stomach.

***

Thinking back on the past three months, a sense of foreboding dimmed Jordan's excitement to meet her husband's new trainee. She'd heard all about the 'new girl', Cassandra, from Adam and his coworkers. Their enthusiasm was intriguing; she'd just graduated from boot camp and was already studying with Adam's department to become a Petty Officer. From what Adam and Danielle had told Jordan about Cassandra, she was a charming, bubbly young woman who was outspoken about her faith. Alex's warning from the night before, however, rang in her mind.

"She's parking now. She'll be right in!" Danielle Meyers called across the restaurant foyer. Jordan, who'd been staring at her engagement and wedding rings on the hand that held her husband's, glanced over Adam's shoulder and smiled at their blonde friend. Her eyes drew back down to their hands, though, when her husband shook his fingers free from hers. Adam didn't spare her a glance, instead strumming those fingers against the wood and downing the last of his beer.

Jordan cleared her throat, shook herself from her thoughts, and jumped up from her stool. Danielle grinned affectionately as she threw her arms around Jordan's shoulders. And just like that, the moment with Adam was forgotten. "I'm sorry I'm late!" a light, gentle voice broke in from the door.

Danielle and Jordan turned, and that foreboding feeling flared in her stomach again. A beautiful petite blonde bounced into the restaurant, glowing like she'd spent her day on the beach. Jordan glanced over to her husband, who was staring at the empty bottle in his hands, before turning back to the woman hugging Danielle.

"Hey, Cassandra, it is so nice to finally meet you!"

"You too, Jordan!" Cassandra pulled her into a hug, and the only word Jordan could use to describe the energy that seemed to surround them was *familiar*...like they had been friends for years.

"Table's ready," Adam interrupted, stepping up and wrapping his arms around Cassandra and lifting her off of her feet. Jordan felt the other woman's eyes on her right away, but Jordan's gaze locked on her shoes. A gentle hand wrapped around her arm, and Danielle tugged her over to the hostess without a word. Jordan heard Cassandra warn Adam that they were going to the table just before she found herself yanked back against his chest.

"You two leaving us behind? Gonna go off and have a date all on your own?" his voice rumbled in her ear. Jordan couldn't help but giggle as his breath tickled her neck, and she leaned against him.

"Oh, you wish," she replied, blowing a teasing kiss at Danielle.

"Hell yeah I do."

***

"So what did you think about Cass?"

Jordan tried not to let her husband calling another woman by a nickname bother her, and focused instead on calling her dog up to the bed. Sammy, a blue-eyed Husky, curled up in her usual spot at the foot of the mattress with her snout resting on Jordan's thigh. Adam settled down on the opposite side of the dog, facing his wife with a childlike smile.

"She seems really sweet," Jordan replied, thinking back on the evening. Despite her best friend's reservations and her husband's strange behavior, Jordan had gotten a strong sense that she was genuinely as focused on her faith as she portrayed herself to be. "It's cool that she's going to the same church.

Maybe now I can get you to join me more often?" She reached over Sammy to poke at her husband, and then nudged the dog out of the way as she leaned over towards him, a playful and tempting smile on her lips.

Adam rolled away from her with a heavy sigh. "You make it sound like I'm into her, like I'm more likely to go because of her than for my own friggin' *wife*? Why do you have to be like that...I'm not in the mood, okay? Let's just get some sleep."

Hurt, but somehow not surprised by his rejection, Jordan withdrew her hand and slowly rolled onto her side, so that they were back-to-back. As the couple fell into tense silence, her mind sifted through memories of similar withdrawals in the time since they were married...taking place more often than not, now that she really considered it. The realization left a gnawing pit in her stomach and tears of self-doubt in her eyes. *What is wrong with me that my own husband hardly ever wants to be with me?* As if sensing her emotions, Sammy whined softly and pressed the length of her body against the back of Jordan's legs.

Adam's familiar snores began, and the brunette knew that she would not be getting any sleep that night; not in their bed, at least. Carefully, she eased herself off of the mattress and padded out of the room, grabbing her robe on the way. Sammy followed, the dog's presence a comfort while she sequestered herself in the living room.

God, I don't know how I keep messing this up. I don't know what to do to make things better with my husband...how to be a better wife. I know that tomorrow it will be as if nothing happened, but I can't keep up with this roller coaster. Give me the strength to press on in this...season of life.

Chapter Two - August

A month later found Jordan, Adam, and their church family at the beach for the annual hangout. Alex and her husband, Brian, chased one another around at the waterline. Jordan giggled as she watched their antics. When she turned towards Adam, prepared to drag him out to join in the fun, she found him laughing along with Cassandra, lost in their own conversation. Her stomach twisted with unease, so she pushed to her feet and made her way down to the water a little way from everyone else to clear her thoughts.

She hated feeling this way; part of her wanted Adam to notice her absence and come after her, another part just needed space. Maybe space would silence Alex's worry, and calm her own churning emotions.

"Jordan!" Sandy, the pastor's wife, caught the brunette's attention with a broad smile and waved her back up to the beach. Jordan complied and noticed a man standing next to her friend. Without having to take a second glance, she could tell he was a Coastie; the hair and posture were all-too-familiar. "I wanted to introduce you to one of our newest visitors! This is Chase; he's in the Coast Guard. I'm not sure if you guys have already met, but I figured you and Adam could bring him into your circle. Maybe have him join your DG?"

Jordan met the newcomer's warm gaze and grinned, offering her hand. "Hey Chase, I'm Jordan." Sandy ducked away with a squeeze of Jordan's shoulder. "My husband Adam is a Health Services Tech at the clinic, what do you do?"

"Nice to meet you, Jordan. I'm a Damage Controlman; firefighter at the station right now. Is your husband on duty today?"

"No, he's right over here with some other Coasties. I'll introduce you." He nodded, and she led the way to their blanket. "Hey hon, guys, got someone new to meet!" Adam and the others turned, and her husband jumped to his feet. Jordan withheld an eye-roll as he straightened to his full height.

"HS2 Adam Davis."

The newcomer shook his hand without flinching, an easy smile on his face. "Chase Falkland. Nice to meet you, man." Jordan watched her husband curiously as Chase explained his position and introduced himself to the rest of the group. Adam turned, quickly shifting to her side and drawing her against him, eyes following the newcomer closely. Alex glanced over and raised a brow at her best friend, but Jordan could only shrug as Adam shifted his arm around her shoulder and laced their fingers together. She hated that she practically preened under his sudden attention.

"So what brought you to our church?" Jordan asked once introductions were over. Everyone settled on Alex and Brian's massive blanket. Adam tugged Jordan to rest back against his chest, catching her off-guard and confirming her suspicions; territorial was not often her husband's M.O.

"I just transferred about a month ago, and I was driving around to get a feel for the area. Saw the sign, decided to check it out, and really enjoyed the whole experience." Chase glanced at Adam for a moment and shrugged. "It's great to find a Gospelteaching church on the first shot. I've definitely been to some doozies after PCSing in the past, ya know?" Cassandra and Jordan chuckled their appreciation for the sentiment. "So Sandy mentioned a DG...what is that exactly?"

Jordan gestured with a sweeping arm to Alex and Brian, the latter of whom responded. "Discipleship Group. Basically, our version of Bible study...Alex and I lead one at our house. We are the unofficial 'Coast Guard group'; even though Lex and I aren't Coasties, Cassandra, Adam and Jordan are part of our group, and there are a few other Coasties as well. We meet on Monday nights, and would love to have you join us."

Adam's arm around her waist tightened fractionally, but he refused to meet her eyes when she shot him a look. She was sure there would be some kind of conversation about this later. "That would be great! I've been looking to get plugged in with some new friends...how many kids do you have?" Chase asked, leaning into the conversation.

"Two," Alex responded, gesturing towards a group of toddlers playing together. "Look for the mops of curly hair, and you've found them." Chase chuckled and nodded.

"We were planning on getting dinner tonight. You wanna join us?" Danielle asked.

Chase considered for a moment. "Why not? I've got nothing else going on." The group continued the conversation until another young couple dragged them into a game of beach volleyball. Jordan attempted to tug Adam along when everyone else jumped up, but he declined, insisting that he was tired and just wanted to watch. Jordan shrugged and left him sprawled out on the blanket to join in with the others.

***

"Okay, okay, okay...so you mean to tell me you prefer being told what to do every single day to being able to do whatever you want?" Kyle - Danielle's boyfriend - questioned, tossing a French fry into his mouth with a grin.

"Well, when you put it *that* way, of course, it sounds insane," Chase responded. Jordan chuckled as he shook his head. He'd settled into the natural rhythm of their group with ease over the course of the day, and had started to open up to them once they made it to dinner at one of her favorite local spots. They'd arrived just in time to claim the seats around a charming fire pit. The sound of the crashing waves and the heat from the fire made for a peaceful, laid-back evening. "But getting paid to help people *and* live near the ocean?"

His smile became nostalgic for a moment. "I grew up in a small town in the middle of nowhere. Going to the beach wasn't really an option, and decent jobs didn't really exist, so joining the Coast Guard and getting away was like a dream. Ship life wasn't the greatest sometimes, but getting to see the world was incredible. And I haven't been here long, but I've been enjoying it so far."

"Even being stuck at the fire station?" Adam chimed in. Jordan glanced over at her husband, who was downing another beer smoothly, and then down at her own mixed drink. *So much for it being his turn to drive...*she thought to herself with an internal sigh.

"Even being 'stuck' at the fire station," Chase agreed. His eyes passed between Adam and Jordan, and she dropped her eyes once more to her drink. "We might not be horribly busy, but we've gotten to go on some pretty intense calls for the city so far as well, so it's been rewarding. What about you guys? What's your experience been like?"

"Well, Davis and I went through A School together before coming here," Danielle offered. "We got here last winter. I met

Kyle a couple of months later. I was on a cutter before school, not a great experience for me. Haven't quite decided how I feel about the clinic so far, but I'm liking Cape May well enough." She smiled tenderly at Kyle, who laced their fingers together before leaning over to kiss her.

"I was at a small boat station up North before school." Adam signaled for another beer. "Met this one through my brother when he dated one of her friends in high school." He gestured to Jordan with his thumb, and the teasing gleam in his eye had her somewhat uneasy. "We grew up in the same hometown. She was crazy enough to put up with my bull, so I figured I had to keep her around. The spring after we got married, we went to Cali for school, and then, like Dani said, we came here. Also not sure how I feel about the clinic, though getting to teach that one over there the ropes has been fun."

Everyone turned to look at Cassandra, Jordan forcing down the sudden ache at the change of tone in her husband's voice when he shifted from talking about her to the petite blonde woman. "Yeah..." Cassandra cleared her throat. "I went through boot camp and went right to the clinic with a couple of other people to learn HS hands-on, so this is my first experience, first station. But I grew up in a beach town, so that part doesn't really phase me. Surfing isn't as good around here, though," she joked. Adam laughed aloud and took a long pull from his new beer.

"Man, I've been trying to get Jordan to surf since we got here, but she's too chicken, aren't you, honey?"

*Nevermind a mildly traumatic childhood experience that justifies being afraid of the ocean...*Alex reached over and squeezed her hand comfortingly, knowing the history behind her fear.

"Surfing isn't for everybody," Cassandra responded lightly. Jordan met her eyes with a grateful smile.

"Yeah, because you need balance to be able to stand up, which we all know Jordy doesn't have." Another beer downed, another stab at her insecurities. Adam started to flag down their waitress again, but this time Chase spoke up, surprising Jordan.

"Actually, man, do you mind if we get the check and head home? I've gotta get ready to stand duty tomorrow." Her husband agreed easily, and the group paid up and was on their way before long.

Danielle and Kyle said their goodbyes; Alex and Brian gave Jordan hugs and welcomed Chase to their little family. Cassandra, Chase, Jordan and Adam made their way to Jordan and Adam's car in silence, until Adam made his way towards the driver's seat.

"Yeah, no...give me the keys. I'm driving," Jordan insisted. Adam tried to argue, but she snatched the keys from him anyway and nudged him towards the passenger's side, knowing he would give up fighting to save face.

"I'm sorry, baby," he cooed once they were in the car. Jordan shook her head, frustrated that he was doing this in front of Cassandra, and Chase, someone they hardly knew. "I know it was supposed to be my night to drive."

"It's fine, Adam. Let's just get everyone home."

"Nuh uh, take me home first. I'm *tired*," he whined. Jordan stared at him incredulously.

"You can easily sleep on the ride. You've done it plenty of times before. It's not fair to-"

"I said take me home first!" Adam growled.

"It's okay, Jordan, it's not too far out of the way, I don't mind. As long as you're good with her taking me home after dropping you and Cassandra off on base?" Chase directed his attention to Adam, who waved a hand with an eye-roll.

"Oh please, she's too much of a goody-two-shoes for me to ever have to worry about her." Jordan was sure that only her husband could so effectively make what should've been a display of trust and love sound biting and snarky when he was drunk.

Tears filled her eyes, and when she glanced in her rearview mirror, Chase's dark gaze caught hers. He tilted his head, and it felt as though he could see right through her, so she shook her head and returned her eyes to the road. Without another word, she made the short drive back to their townhome at the base housing and then dropped Cassandra off at the barracks.

With just the two of them in the car, it felt weird to have Chase in the back seat. "Do you want to move up front? It'll make it easier for you to give me directions anyway," Jordan murmured, refusing to take her eyes off of the steering wheel as she spoke. Chase moved without verbally responding and gave her basic directions to start.

They made most of the drive in silence, with Chase stealing glances at her and Jordan pretending she didn't notice. The man unsettled her; despite the fact that she'd just met him earlier in the day, the problem wasn't the fact that they were alone. It was the fact that she felt safe having *just met him*, and the fact that he was looking at her like he *got* her.

Alex was the only person who'd done the same from the moment they'd met. Which was why they'd been best friends most of their lives, and why Alex and Brian had moved to Cape May to live near them. She wasn't sure what to do with possibly having a man other than her husband being able to read her so well.

"Does he often drink like that while you guys are out?" His voice was even, no sign of judgment evident as his gaze remained steady on her.

Well, no beating around the bush tonight, I guess. Jordan sighed and took a moment to answer, trying to figure out how to do so gracefully. "I'm sorry he was so rude. Work's been stressing him out." Her excuse fell flat, and she had to bite her tongue to keep from filling that space with everything that she was feeling...her frustration towards Adam for drinking too much, her insecurities about her marriage, her embarrassment that this is his first impression of her and her husband.

"That why he was so snarky towards you all night?" He pointed out his house as Jordan turned onto his street.

Jordan pulled into his driveway, threw the vehicle into park, and turned in her seat to stare at him with a raised brow when he made no move to leave her car, still waiting for her answer. "Are you usually this upfront with people the day you meet them?" As much as she tried to inject some bite into her words, there was only sincerity in her voice, to her deep annoyance.

Chase softened at her question and gave her a wry smile. "You're right, I'm sorry. No, I'm not usually so nosy until I've gotten to know someone." He unbuckled his seatbelt. As he reached for the door, he hesitated and turned back to look at her. "I don't know the state of your marriage, but I *do* know that you deserve to be treated with a hell of a lot more respect than your husband showed tonight. Goodnight, Jordan. Thank you for bringing me home."

It took every ounce of willpower to keep her tears at bay as she nodded to him, and only by the grace of God did she hold out until Chase was inside before breaking down into sobs.

Chapter Three
-Chase-

"Thanks for driving, man. I can't stand trying to park in this madness. Especially when it means having to concentrate over the dull roar in the backseat." Chase Falkland glanced at his passenger and then back over his shoulder to the three women chatting happily in the backseat of his Wrangler. He grinned wryly and shrugged.

"I've had to drive in much crazier places and much less maneuverable vehicles, so this doesn't bother me. Besides, it only made sense that we take one vehicle since everyone can fit into mine." Everyone jumped out once he parked, and Chase drew a deep inhale. Fried food, waffle cones, and the bite of saltwater invaded his senses, and he couldn't help feeling like a little kid going on a brand-new adventure.

"First time making it out to the boardwalk?" Danielle questioned with a grin. She, Cassandra and Jordan were standing arm-in-arm, clearly waiting for him to get moving. Adam had gone off to pay the parking lot attendant.

"Yeah, actually. It's been so crazy getting settled in and qualified at the firehouse that I just haven't been able to make time to check out tourist stuff outside of Cape May." The group started for the boardwalk once Adam returned. "I didn't realize just how different Wildwood is from Cape May...and this isn't like anything I've ever gotten to experience before."

As they stepped into the crowd, surrounded by shops, Chase took a moment to soak in the experience: the bass of a hip-hop song reverberating from a nearby t-shirt shop, the giggles of children on rides at the pier across the way, the overall bustle of hundreds of visitors spending time with loved ones.

It was something to behold, that was certain...but not necessarily something he'd be eager to behold on a regular basis in the height of summer. Growing up in a small town had helped Chase to appreciate the quiet, the calm...he'd seen the busyness of Cape May in his short time at the Training Center, but the Wildwood boardwalk was a different story altogether.

"Give it a couple of weeks. Once Labor Day hits, things slow down and we get to appreciate this stuff without the insanity." Jordan's amused voice drew him from his thoughts. He looked up to see her standing in front of a store with Adam's arm thrown around her shoulder and an understanding in her eyes that was somewhat unsettling. "This tends to be too much for me too, most days...I recognize that look." Adam gave a subtle eye-roll and turned away. Jordan pulled herself free from his grasp and turned to watch him start down the boardwalk with the rest of their group. Chase stepped up alongside her and wondered at the man's demeanor.

"I take it he's more of an extrovert?"

Jordan grinned up at him, but her eyes were somewhat guarded. Not for the first time, he wondered how much went on behind the scenes in their relationship...how much of the distance was Jordan's nature, and how much came from the behaviors he'd only glimpsed in the brief time he'd known the Davises.

The bright light Chase had seen in her eyes, her welcoming nature when they'd first met, led him to believe that there was more than just innate insecurity behind the subtle shifts. "Definitely more so than me, but when it comes to crowds it honestly doesn't take much. I wouldn't have pegged *you* for an introvert, though."

Chase laughed, and gestured for them to catch up to the others. "With most things I'm not, but growing up in a small town made me much more comfortable with a slower pace of life. This kind of chaos is not something I was quite prepared for."

"You start to get used to it, I promise. It's definitely an overwhelming event the first time around." They followed along behind Adam, Danielle, and Cassandra, with Chase taking in the sights as they went.

"You know, I just realized after getting to know more about what they all do the other night, I never learned about you," Chase commented. She glanced at him, surprise clear on her face for a fleeting second. "What?"

Jordan shook her head with a self-deprecating laugh. "Sorry, sometimes you military guys surprise me when you are actually interested in learning anything about us spouses. We tend to be invisible." Chase shook his head, disappointed but unsurprised by the sentiment.

"Well, you're not invisible to me. So, how do you keep yourself busy while your husband is off playing military?"

Jordan smiled. "I work at an inpatient psychiatric facility, and am in grad school online right now to become a therapist."

Her answer caught him off guard, and he shook his head with a huff of laughter. "That's impressive. What's it like working at the inpatient facility?"

"It's really rewarding to get to see some of the patients progress from really dark places, to being able to step down to lower levels of care. There are some that have more down days than up, and those days can get pretty intense, but overall I love what I do." Her smile became shy, so he decided to let the conversation settle for the moment.

As they passed a shop with dresses and shirts he noticed Jordan reach out and absently skim her fingertips along each article, and he wondered if she even realized what she was doing. With each store she did the same thing, until he finally couldn't withhold his curiosity anymore.

"Sorry...did you want to stop and look at anything?"

Jordan glanced at him, and then down at her hand. Red colored the tips of her ears as she tangled her fingers behind her back with a sheepish grin. "No! No, I'm good, sorry...I like to feel the different textures." She shrugged. "It's just something I've always done, pretty much everywhere I go that sells clothing."

"You two coming or what? We've decided we're getting food first, Hurry it up!" Adam called from a few storefronts ahead. Jordan looked over to him and nodded, but Chase kept his eyes on her, watching the subtle shift of her posture and demeanor. She seemed to hesitate, so he started off towards the pizza parlor behind Adam and the other women. As she turned away from the store something seemed to catch her eye and she halted.

"Ooh, Adam, wait just a second! I've been looking for one of these for ages!" Chase grinned at the excitement in her voice, but when he glanced back to their companions, they were already heading into the restaurant. The fireman shook his head, torn between jogging to them and asking them to wait and following Jordan into the store.

She solved the debate for him a moment later, though, when she pranced back out to the sunlight. Bright, vibrant joy dimmed instantly when she saw that they were gone. For a beat, Chase swore there were tears in her eyes. As soon as she blinked, however, they were gone, and a wide grin - too wide, and not reflected in her eyes - shone at him.

"They, uh, they went inside. Did you get what you were looking for?"

Jordan cleared her throat. "No, I don't...it wasn't what I thought it was," she replied nonchalantly. "I should've just waited 'til after we ate. If we don't hurry up, they'll eat all the pizza before we even get there. Come on, better fuel up if you're going to survive your first boardwalk adventure." She strode past him, refusing to look him in the eye, and kept her chin raised proudly.

Chase sighed, but followed along without further comment. Once they made it to the restaurant, he held the door for her. Jordan smiled gratefully, but faltered when she looked inside. He followed her gaze to see Adam, Cassandra and Danielle chatting and joking as though their absence wasn't even noticed.

Chapter Four - September

Jordan's knee bounced anxiously as she waited for her husband to walk through the door. She'd gotten dressed and ready for their planned outing to Atlantic City an hour before, and had only to wait for him to get home (an hour late so far) and ready himself before they would be out the door. Alex, Brian, and Chase all waited for the go-ahead to leave as well, knowing better than to count on the military to leave on time. Jordan smiled to herself as she thought of her friends, grateful for their presence in her life and excited to spend the evening celebrating her birthday with them.

The door finally opening drew the brunette from her thoughts, and Adam stepped in with a smile on his face - until he looked up and saw his wife's face. "Oh, shoot, Jor, I forgot to text you and tell you that Danielle and Cassandra can't make it tonight...I meant to tell you to go with Alex and the guys without us."

Jordan canted her head, her stomach twisting with dread. "Us? Adam, you're home now, even if they can't make it. Why don't we just finish getting ready and head out? There's still plenty of time," she pointed out. Adam sighed heavily and started untying his black work boots.

"Look, I just don't feel like going all the way to AC tonight, okay? It's been a really freakin' long day, and I want to play some music and go to sleep."

Anger flared at his words. "I had a long day at work too, Adam. D-do you even remember *why* we had plans to go out tonight?" A single sharp look squashed Jordan's anger, replacing it with that all-too-familiar dread. "Please, Adam...it's my birthday. I don't even care if we stay local at this point, just...can we please go out? Everyone else is going to be concerned if you don't come with me."

"Fine! Figure out somewhere around here to go. Might as well let Danielle and Cass know about the change of plans while you're at it." He tossed his boots against the wall roughly and stomped up the stairs, either not noticing or not reacting to Jordan's flinch. The bedroom door slammed, causing another involuntary flinch before Jordan took a steadying breath.

Ignoring the burning in her eyes, she pulled out her phone and texted the others to let them know about the change of plans.

'Sounds good, see you guys in an hour?' -Chase

'I'm sensing some tension, what's up?' -Alex

'Dani, Kyle and I will definitely be there!' -Cassandra

Jordan read each response as they came in, but couldn't bring herself to reply to any of them. Where she'd just been excited moments before about celebrating her birthday, suddenly *she* was the one lacking the desire to be around people. Her best friend would see right through her. Chase would innocently ask why plans changed, and whatever excuse Adam gave would raise alarms in Alex's head.

The sound of doors opening and closing and the shower water starting to run let Jordan know that she had at least twenty minutes before her husband was even to the point of getting dressed, so she snatched up Sammy's leash and took the dog out into the cool evening air.

Before she'd made it a block, her cell started to ring. Her best friend's face grinned up at her from the screen, and Jordan steeled herself before answering. "Hey, Lex, it'll probably be an hour before we're ready."

"Don't pretend you don't know why I'm calling, Jordan. Are you inside?"

"No," Jordan sighed. "I'm taking Sammy for a walk while he's in the shower." There was a breath of hesitation before she finally let go of the tight grip on her emotions. "He came home an hour late, and had completely forgotten about dinner. Danielle and Cassandra had canceled, too. It...it wasn't until I mentioned what you guys would think that Adam even agreed to go somewhere local."

"Oh, Jordan, I'm sorry," Alex murmured. Jordan blinked away tears, determined not to let her makeup get ruined and alert her husband to her pain. "Are you sure *you're* up for this?"

A humorless laugh erupted from the brunette. "Not exactly like I can back out now, can I? Adam would throw a *fit*. I just...want to get through tonight. By the time we get there, I'll be fine, have a couple of drinks, and pretend like this was the plan all along. No big deal."

"Jordan..."

"It's fine, Alex, *I'm* fine. I'll see you at the restaurant in an hour." Before her friend could respond, Jordan hung up and turned back home.

The drive to the restaurant was as tense as she expected it to be, so Jordan decided that she needed to extend the olive branch. "I'm sorry that I bombarded you when you got home. Thank you for being willing to come out, anyway."

Adam remained silent for a moment before finally responding. "Like you said, it's your birthday. We'll still have fun, I promise." He grinned, and Jordan felt the tension in her muscles release a fraction.

Once they made it to their destination, Jordan took a deep breath and followed Adam inside. Danielle, Kyle and Cassandra were already seated, and a big bouquet of flowers with a card sat on the place setting next to Cassandra. Jordan smiled as their friends jumped up to give her hugs. As they settled, Chase arrived, followed shortly by Alex and Brian. Alex gave Jordan an extra squeeze before taking the seat beside her husband. She allowed herself to make the most of the evening, ignoring the nagging voice in the back of her mind that Adam was acting strangely.

***

"Babe, why don't we go get lunch? I'm starving...maybe at that place by the bridge?" Jordan looked over to her husband, her smile faltering when she saw the annoyed look in his eyes.

"We just went out last night," Adam muttered under his breath. He glanced around at the lingering churchgoers and ducked out of the building with no further goodbyes. Jordan took a deep breath to push back the tears suddenly pricking her eyes. She waved to Michelle, and whispered goodbye to Alex and Brian. Her best friend stepped forward, concerned, but Jordan shook her head firmly.

"I'm fine," she insisted. She knew if she said something, she'd get emotional, and that would just set off Adam. "I'll see you tomorrow."

With that, she jogged out to catch up to her husband. "Adam, Adam, wait up! Yeah, we went out as a group, for my *birthday*...not without some resistance on your part, I might add. But when was the last time we went out, just the two of us? You've been so busy with work that it feels like we haven't seen each other in two weeks." Frustration and sadness welled up in her when he got into their car without responding. She followed suit, torn between wanting to curl up in a ball or shake her husband until he explained why he'd been so distant lately. "Adam, please-"

"Jesus Christ, Jordan, would you give it a rest for two damn seconds?!" The brunette's mouth closed with an audible 'smack' and she stared at Adam, surprised by his outburst. "Way to nearly cause a scene in front of everyone in there, by the way."

Fear and dread settled into her stomach at the cold glare he gave her. "W-what?" she stuttered, "I...A-Adam, I didn't-"

"I think it's time to put this on the table. It's been there, dangling over our heads, for months, you and I both know it. We need to get a divorce."

Had she not already been sitting, Jordan was sure she'd have fallen over. Nausea turned her stomach at the words, and shock silenced any and all thought except for *No...nononono...* "W-what?!"

Chapter Five

"Oh, come on, don't pretend like you haven't thought about it yourself," Adam scoffed as he pulled out of the parking lot. "Things have been bad for a while now; you can't tell me that it hasn't bothered you."

Finally finding her voice through the shock and around the lump forming in her throat, Jordan shook her head. "Of course it's *bothered* me, Adam, but seriously? *Divorce*? What happened to 'we don't believe in it' and not using that against each other?" Anger and fear warred in her chest when she looked over and saw the nonchalance on his face.

"Stop being dense, Jordan. There's not really much to say that'll change anything at this point. It's been a long time coming." He glanced over at her with a smirk. "I'm sure *Chase* will be thrilled to hear the news, and he'll be happy to help you move on."

Anger won out with a blaze. "Don't you dare drag him into this. It has *never* been like that with Chase and you damn well know it. You-" She cut herself off before finishing the sentence, knowing it would only make him angry to point out how many times he left her in a position to have done anything with Chase in the first place.

"Maybe not, but it doesn't mean that he doesn't *want* it to be."

Jordan took a deep, steadying breath and forced herself to let the issue go. "No matter what you think, this is the farthest thing from what I want." She thought for a moment. "If we're going to do this, I want to go to counseling first. We have to at least try to fix it."

"I mean, it's not going to get us anywhere, but fine. I've been thinking about it for a while; it was the reason everyone tried to back out last night. They wanted me to handle it sooner rather than dragging it out." The scenery passing by was as much of a blur as the thoughts in her mind as she struggled to process what he'd just revealed, and before she knew it Adam had pulled up in front of their townhome. "Look, I'm going to go for a drive for a while. By myself."

Jordan stared at her hands, clenched in her lap, for a moment before giving a humorless laugh and shaking her head. Without a word she got out of their SUV, gazing numbly after it as her husband pulled away in an agonizing representation of their life. She hurried inside before the dam holding back her emotions finally broke, and she found herself on her knees on the living room floor.

Sammy whined, nudging her with her nose, and Jordan buried her face in the dog's fur as sobs wracked her body. *God, this can't be real. I can't do this...I can't handle this. Please wake me up from this nightmare. Take this burden from me, because right now I feel like I'm crumbling under the weight. I feel so desperately alone...I need Your arms to wrap around me.*

Though it felt like an eternity that she spent weeping against Sammy, when Jordan pulled out her phone to call her best friend she realized that only ten minutes had passed. Before she could hit 'call', though, nerves won out and she resorted to texting Alex instead. Within minutes, a knock at the front door drew her attention, and she pushed herself against the couch to stand.

"Okay, talk to me. What's going on?"

Jordan took a shuddering breath and gestured outside. "Can we go to the lighthouse first? I don't want to be here right now." Alex nodded, confusion settling into her eyes.

***

"Brian's going to kill him," Alex growled, running her fingers through Sammy's fur to keep herself calm.

"No, he can't. I don't want this to be a big thing just yet. He agreed to counseling, so...it still might work out." Even as she said the words though, Jordan didn't believe them. "Cassandra and Danielle knew he was going to ask. That's why they tried to bail yesterday. They wanted him to do it then."

"On your *birthday?!* Please tell me you're kidding? What...why...I just can't..." She trailed off, shaking her head angrily. "I'm sorry, Jordy. What can I do?"

"Just, remind *me* not to kill him too sometimes?" They both gave wet laughs. "And don't tell anyone besides Brian."

Alex nodded. "Of course. No matter what, we'll get through this. I've got you. God's got you." She wrapped an arm around Jordan's shoulder, and Jordan leaned into her best friend's embrace, allowing tears to fall again as they lapsed into a heavy silence.

***

The first marriage counseling homework assignment found Jordan and Adam sharing dinner at a small, quiet pub. Jordan picked at a pulled pork sandwich, appetite virtually non-existent in the week since Adam turned her life upside-down.

"Look, I know you don't believe in counseling, but if we have any hope of fixing this, I think this is the only way to do it. She wanted us to talk, to see if there was anything still there, so...what's on your mind right now?" she asked, voice soft and timid.

Adam chuckled, the sound hollow and devoid of humor, and watched her with a raised eyebrow. She felt minuscule under his scrutiny, and for the first time wondered if, maybe, her life would be better if they got divorced. "No matter how much counseling we go to, no matter how many dates we go on trying to tell ourselves that we can fix this, we can't. I'm in love with her."

As much as the confession felt like a suckerpunch, Jordan found herself laughing humorlessly as well. There was no need to question who 'she' was; she'd known the day she met Cassandra - the beautiful, petite paramedic who Adam was training - that her husband would be intrigued by her. Not much of a stretch for him to want her, and convince himself he was in love with her.

"I can't say I'm surprised. That's it for counseling, huh?" She was silent for a moment, picking at her food. "This isn't what I want. I would still work to fix this, but I will not beg you to stay, Adam." The strength in her voice surprised Jordan, considering the pounding of her heart and tremor in her hands. She knew it was only by the grace of God that she was staying strong...that she'd hold it together until she was away from him.

Chapter Six - October

The month following the spectacular failure of their attempt at marriage counseling had been somewhat torturous for Jordan. Adam had, for all intents and purposes, went on behaving as though their marriage hadn't dissolved under their feet; he continued to hug her when he got home (even if it was ridiculously late most nights), invited her to practice music with him in their downtime, and challenged her any time she brought up the idea of telling the church family the truth of their situation. Alex had been her rock through the process, but she wasn't sure that she could handle much more pretending that everything was fine.

Seeing Cassandra tore at her heart - Adam swore that she had no idea of his feelings for her, and of course the other woman (just like everyone else) had no idea that they were separating. Her eternal optimism usually lifted Jordan's spirits, but when that optimism turned towards the topic of her marriage, she found herself wishing the earth would open up under her feet.

"Jordan, hey...just got orders for pharmacy school in Texas. I head out next week, and will be gone until March." *Wow...well that's one way to make the separation happen.*

The brunette looked up from her desk to see Adam standing in the doorway to their spare room with a broad smile on his face. She nodded, unsure of how to respond.

Apparently, a lack of response was not correct. Adam rolled his eyes and sighed heavily. "You'd think this news would've made you happy, would've been what you *wanted*."

With that single sentence, a month's worth of anger crashed over her at once. Jordan scoffed. "Yeah, Adam, you going away and giving us the *separation* that *you asked for* a month ago because you are *in love with someone else* is exactly what I want!" She shoved away from the desk and stepped up to him. Surprise was clear in his eyes for a moment, before indignation quickly took its place. "What I *wanted* was for you not to destroy our lives, and then *pretend* like nothing had changed. This?" Her laugh was somewhat hysterical as she gestured around them. "*This* has been my own personal hell. So forgive me if I'm not jumping for joy at your new orders, Adam."

"Wow, nice to see some fire for once," he teased with a smirk. He glanced down at his watch. "Isn't group tonight? What are you still doing here?"

The abrupt change of direction disoriented her for half a beat. "I was waiting for you to get home. You've gone with me the last two weeks and put on a happy face, why would I have expected tonight to be any different?"

"Well, you're going to have to go without me tonight. I'm tired, it's been a long day."

Jordan shook her head again and dropped her chin to her chest. "Thanks for letting me know. I'll be back later." She took a deep breath to bolster her resolve. "And I think I'm going to sleep in the guest room until you leave. I'll take Sammy with me tonight. She hasn't seen the kids in a while." With that, she brushed past Adam and made it out the door with dog in tow, *before* tears managed to win out over her determination to be strong.

By the time she made it to Alex and Brian's house, it was clear by the laughter drifting through the windows that the group had already started. *God, give me strength.* With a steadying breath, Jordan opened the door of her Jeep and allowed Sammy out behind her. She poked her head over the fence as she opened the gate just enough to let Sammy into the yard, and waved with a grin at the kids now running for the dog.

The group looked up at her as she entered her best friend's house, and both Alex and Chase grew serious as they took in her demeanor. "Hey guys, sorry I'm late. Adam got home late from work and was too tired to come with." Cassandra gave her an odd look, and suddenly she had the strength to speak the truth. "I've got something to share...Adam asked me for a divorce about a month ago."

Alex stood and hugged her immediately. "I'm so proud of you." Jordan smiled weakly, and Alex led her to an empty spot on the couch.

"Are you okay?" Chase asked softly from across the living room. The compassion in his voice, and knowledge that she was safe with her closest friends surrounding her, broke through Jordan's defenses, and tears started falling once more. Alex laced their fingers together and tugged Jordan to rest her head on her shoulder, and Jordan began to explain the (abridged) events of the previous month.

* * *

The week between Adam getting his orders and actually leaving had been a new level of difficult; gone was the false sense of stability. Instead, Adam had become angry and argumentative in a way Jordan had not experienced before. He'd left her with the insistence that she be moved out before he came back, and suddenly the prospect of her marriage actually ending was all too real.

Without thinking twice after he was gone, she summoned her husky and went to her safe space. As she sat down on the cool sand in front of the lighthouse, thoughts of the first day that she met Cassandra passed through her mind. As though those memories summoned her, an all-too-familiar voice broke her reverie.

"Hey girly, whatcha thinkin about?" Jordan looked up into the warm, bubbly face of her friend. She smiled back at Cassandra, and settled onto her elbows. The blonde woman lowered herself to sit on the sand, and fussed over the dark husky curled between them.

Jordan ran her fingers through Sammy's fur. "Just remembering the day we met, actually. Crazy to think how much life can change in four months." The women looked at one another, Jordan with watery eyes and a tremulous smile. Cassandra dropped her gaze and shook her head.

"I still can't believe what Adam did. He had everything going for him...he had a good life."

"Some people will never be satisfied, I guess." *If only you knew just what he'd gone and done.*

"Have you figured out yet what you're going to do?" she asked. Jordan stared out at the waves for a long moment before she responded.

"Keep praying, follow whatever God has planned from here. I can't say it's anything new, being the last to know and therefore the one left scrambling to clean up the mess. Kind of his M.O. the last few years in particular, so I've gotten pretty good at damage control." Cassandra winced and bit her bottom lip, and guilt settled into Jordan's stomach. "I'm sorry, it's too beautiful a day for me to be such a downer. Let's talk about something else."

"Okay, how about all of the new Coasties coming to church lately? It's pretty awesome to see so many people starting to attend." She grinned. "Any of them catch your eye?"

The question caught Jordan off guard; her papers weren't even *filed* yet. "It's only been a month since he asked for the divorce. I haven't even processed what all of this means for us. For *me*. It'll be a long time until I can even think about someone catching my eye, and who knows how long this is going to take." Even as their conversation continued, Jordan couldn't shake the uneasiness brought about by Cassandra's bizarre timing.

Chapter Seven - March

"So how is the new house treating you and Sammy?" Cassandra asked between bites of salad. Jordan smiled tiredly, thinking back on the two weeks of adjusting and unpacking since their discipleship group moved all of her things out of the home she'd shared with Adam and into her own space.

"It's been great. Finally getting out of a house that had too many memories and was so close to everyone that just reminds me of Adam has been a huge relief." The brunette shrugged. "Unpacking has been tough at times, I've gotta admit; I've found a few wedding pieces that just felt like a knife to the chest."

Cassandra reached out and squeezed her hand. "I'm sorry it's been hard for you."

"It's all part of the process, I know, but I don't think I'm quite ready to let some of that stuff go, you know what I mean? I don't want to get rid of something out of pain or anger now, and regret it later. I think it'll be important one day to have the reminder that it wasn't all bad." Cassandra nodded.

Jordan chewed on her lip, debating whether she should share her next thought. "He had me questioning my sanity when he got back," she murmured, eyes locked on her plate as she spoke. "The whole reason I moved when I did was because he demanded that I be gone before he got back, remember? Well, I was informed of his return by a text about how I was a coward for leaving and denying that it was his choice in the first place." A wry, bitter grin tugged at her lips. "Thankfully, I'd kept all of his messages, because that was the only proof I had that it wasn't all in my head." When she finally looked up at Cassandra, the other woman looked desperately uncomfortable.

"So, Adam is back at work and refuses to talk to anyone about what's going on. Makes for pretty awkward break conversations when no one has seen him in five months." The pitch to her friend's voice was several steps higher than normal, and Jordan resisted the urge to flinch.

"Oh, yeah?"

"Mhm," Cassandra hummed while she chewed. "He looks stressed, a lot more than when I saw him a couple of months ago," she added.

It took a moment for the words to sink in, for the *meaning* behind the words to sink in, but as she stared at Cassandra the other woman simply continued eating, oblivious to the slip.

"A...a couple m-months ago?" The fork fell out of Jordan's trembling fingers with a loud clatter, and the heat of humiliation rushed to her face. Finally, Cassandra looked at her, and realization dawned in her eyes.

"Uh, yeah. Adam came home over Christmas while you were visiting your parents," she murmured, setting her own fork down gently. The woman's eyes darted all over the room, refusing to meet Jordan's gaze again.

"He...he didn't say anything to me about that." *How would he have known it was even safe to come back, considering they didn't talk while he was gone?* "How did he know I wouldn't be around? There's," she shook her head, "there's *no way* he would have come back if he hadn't known what I was doing." The guilt that took over Cassandra's face and seemed to settle like a weight on the woman's shoulders told Jordan more than enough, and she felt nauseous. "You were talking to him while he was away."

"H-he reached out, said that he needed someone to talk to because everyone else just seemed too close to the situation, so he couldn't talk to them," Cassandra whispered. Jordan's jaw clenched as she processed the feeble attempt at justification.

"He couldn't talk to one of our friends that doesn't talk to me anymore, but he could reach out to the *one* mutual friend that does, and is *arguably* closest to the situation? And you were perfectly content to talk to him, knowing full well that he had completely shut me out...and *hid it from me*? How long before he came home?"

The blonde picked at her napkin. "Maybe a week before Christmas."

"He 'needed someone to talk to' a week before he came back; more like he needed to keep tabs on what I was doing so he knew if it was safe to come home, and he knew that no one else would have much of a clue anymore. You should have *told* me." Horror settled into her chest as a sick sense of understanding finally began to sink in. "Except...you *saw him* when he came back."

"Jordan, look-"

Jordan shoved away from the table, shaking her head and willing herself not to cry in front of Cassandra. "No. No, no. I don't want to hear whatever excuse you are about to give me. One of the people that understands everything and talked me through so much, w-was talking to *my husband* and *met up with my husband* behind my back while he and I weren't even *speaking*. You've led me to believe this whole time that you had no idea how he felt about you." Tears burned her eyes at that realization. "I believed our friendship meant more, that this was a line that you *never* would have crossed. Nothing you can say to me will ever make this okay."

Without a second glance, Jordan clutched her purse to her chest and hurried away, only stopping long enough to give some money to the hostess before rushing towards her car. Sammy whined at her from the front seat as she climbed in, providing enough of a distraction for Jordan to focus on getting out of the parking lot and driving the blessedly short distance to her safe haven.

The sound of waves crashing against the sand and the scent of salt water did little to soothe her devastation. After six months, she hadn't thought things could get any worse, and still the shock of betrayal from both her husband and now one of her closest friends felt like a white-hot knife between her ribs. It stole her breath and burned in her eyes. Jordan dropped onto her back, her arm falling to cover her eyes as a sob rose from her chest. Her husky whined and dropped her head onto Jordan's stomach. The brunette muttered an *'oof'* of surprise and chuckled wetly.

"I know, I'm sorry. It's just been a rough day." She reached down and scratched behind Sammy's ears, opening her eyes again to stare at the sky. "What are we going to do about this mess that has become my life? Huh, Sammy?"

She shook her head wryly, and sighed. "I need You to show me what I'm supposed to do here, God. I'm feeling really lost...I don't want to go back home after You just provided me with my own space, but I can't keep this up forever. It's safe to say my feet are failing me. Tell me," her voice turned desperate and tears blurred her vision, "tell me what I'm supposed to do. Tell me who I'm supposed to trust, because right now it feels like I've got no one."

"Jay?" Sammy jumped up, instantly alert and taking a protective stance over her owner. A familiar figure approached from the water. "Jordan, hey! I-" He faltered when he saw the expression on Jordan's face, "I'm sorry if I'm interrupting something, but, hi," he finished lamely.

Jordan nudged Sammy forward so she could sit up, and smiled in spite of herself at the intruder (Jordan realized she did *not* object to this particular intrusion). She cleared her throat and blinked away her tears. "Hey, Chase. No, it's okay. Perfect timing, really. Did you catch any good waves?" She gestured with a tilt of her head to the surfboard tucked securely under his arm.

Chase looked down at the board, then down to the wetsuit protecting him from the elements as though he'd forgotten they were there, and flashed her a charming smile. "I got a few, yeah. It was a good day to spend some quiet time out there with God, ya know?" He perched his board upright in the sand, still standing far enough back to not invade the dog's comfort zone. "So, this is Sammy?"

"This is Sammy, *Samantha*." Fingers ruffled fur before pointing to Chase. "Sammy, this is Chase. Go say hi, he's a friend." Like a switch had been flipped, the husky's tail swished back and forth and she bounded up to him. Chase chuckled as he crouched to meet her.

"Well hello there, *Samantha*. It's nice to finally meet you," Chase murmured. Sammy sniffed his face before dragging her tongue along his cheek. Deep, rich laughter rang through the air, and Jordan grinned. "She's awesome."

"Yeah, I like to think so," she teased. "Thank you." The two shared a long gaze, before he searched her face.

"What's wrong?" he finally asked, voice gentle and serious once more.

Her smile faltered, and she turned her gaze to the waves. Chase had come to town eight months ago, swooped into her church and ingrained himself in their lives seamlessly. She was intrigued by him from the moment they'd met, but their friendship had been a slow build. Even still...he'd had an uncanny ability to read her from the start. She didn't think she was ready to open up to him yet about what had just turned her world upside down, so she simply shrugged.

"It's just been one of those days." Chase didn't respond for a long moment, so she turned her focus back to him. Concern seeped into his now-serious face, but he still didn't speak. Jordan quirked a half-smile. "I'm fine," she assured, "just had my own bit of quiet time with God."

Chase considered her for another moment, clearly unconvinced. "Alright, Davis. If you say so." He kissed Sammy on the snout. "I've gotta head back. See you Sunday?" Jordan nodded. Chase reached forward and squeezed her shoulder. "You know how to reach me if you need anything."

"Thank you, Chase. I'll see you later." Both Jordan and Sammy watched as he scooped up his surfboard, waved, and jogged up the path to the street. The young woman sighed and dropped her forehead to her dog's shoulder. "Why can't more guys be genuinely nice like him?"

Sammy gave a low whine, and settled down into the sand. Jordan nodded, and rolled back to lay in the sand again with a heavy sigh. She was grateful for the fact that the beach was so empty in the offseason. It allowed her to stay there, watching the colors float through the spectrum as the sun slipped below the horizon, without further distraction. There had been many times where being alone with her thoughts would have terrified her, but finally Jordan was finding solace in her solitude once again. When she was alone, she could direct her heart and her attention to God; to finally rebuild the relationship she'd drifted from for much of the last seven years.

After taking time to talk to God, Jordan pulled out her phone. Nerves nearly got the best of her as her fingers hovered over the keyboard, thinking of half a dozen potential outcomes (and none of them pleasant), but a gentle breeze ruffled her hair and soothed her. *Thank you, Lord.*

'The papers can be filed now. I can have a friend from church pick them up or meet you somewhere and then I'll mail them in myself. When is a good day for you?'

The response took what felt like ages to come, and when it did, dread settled into her chest. 'workin on it. txt u when its done.'

She had a battle ahead.

Chapter Eight - June

"God, I ask that you reveal to each of us the idols in our hearts. Help us to surrender those idols to you, and redirect that worship to you, where it belongs. In Jesus' name we pray...amen." Pastor David looked up to his congregation, and waved with a smile. "You guys are dismissed, have a great week!"

Jordan took a deep breath, and slid her microphone back into its stand. She tugged her ear monitors free, and grinned at her teammates. They quietly shuffled off of the stage, and Jordan headed for her seat. As she walked, she wound the wire for her monitors and tucked them into their case. Jordan prepared to leave, eager to get out on the water after a long winter season, until a shadow crossed her vision and drew her gaze.

"You sounded great today, Davis."

A shy smile tugged at her lips as she slid her purse onto her shoulder. "Thank you, Falkland," she responded. Nervous energy thrummed through her, and she couldn't discern whether it was lingering from singing, or from the man standing before her.

The draw to Chase was undeniable in moments like this, but her pending divorce hung over her like a heavy-laden storm cloud. They had become even closer friends in the three months since Adam's return, and Chase had been nothing if not respectful to her. As much as she fought to keep her thoughts from wandering towards what a relationship with him would be like, she failed; particularly when he looked at her with a tender smile that made her believe she wasn't alone in her feelings.

"Jay?" *Whoops.* "You okay?" The way his smile morphed into an almost-smug grin spoke volumes, and heat burned in her cheeks.

"Uh," she huffed a laugh. "yeah, sorry. What was that?"

"What are your plans for the rest of the day?" Jordan took a moment, debating whether she should open a door she knew she wouldn't have the willpower to close. It was one thing to grab lunch with a friend, but sharing her favorite and most personal past time with someone who could appreciate how significant it was? That would bring him into a deeper level of her life than she could come back from.

And yet, that same pull that drew her to him anytime he was in her vicinity made the thought of keeping that part of herself walled off to him feel *wrong*. "I'm-" She hesitated for another moment, thinking of all the times she had been hurt and let down before. "I'm taking advantage of the first gorgeous Sunday of the year and getting myself out on the water." She forced herself to look into his eyes and hoped she was right about him. "Interested?"

The wide, beaming smile was all the answer she needed, and warmth spread through her at the confirmation. Case told her to give him fifteen minutes to run home and grab his board. Jordan shook her head and chuckled to herself: "you're so in trouble, Davis." She sighed as she watched him go. She waved to her friends as she jogged out to her car, grabbing her suit to get changed while she waited for him to return.

***

"How have you never been out here before?" Chase asked incredulously. Jordan glanced over to him as she waded into the water. "You've lived here much longer than I have!" A good-natured eye roll earned her a laugh, and she turned back to make sure she was out far enough to drop her board into the water. She took a moment to adjust once she was on the paddle board, and then eased herself to her feet as she had a thousand times. The sway of the waves felt comforting. Familiar.

"You realize that we live at the *beach*, right? That miles of shorelines and inlets surround us from three sides? Next time I'll show you some of *my* favorite spots. How did you-*really*, Falkland?"

Even on the shore, she could see the mirth sparkling in his chocolate eyes. "What, I'm not allowed to take my time?"

"Not when you have to show me what makes this place so much better than my favorite spot, no! Get your lazy bones *out* here!" Jordan gestured animatedly with her paddle, secretly celebrating when she maintained her balance with no outward difficulty. Chase's laughter as he complied and jogged out to meet her warmed her cheeks, and she watched as he stood himself up as well. Sunlight glinted off of the rivulets tracing his chest and abs. Jordan had to close her eyes and remind herself that, though she was separated, she was still *technically* married.

"Hey," his smooth voice hummed beside her. Jordan's eyes snapped open, and he reached out to steady her when her board wobbled violently. "It's time for you to get out of that head of yours for a little while, hm?" When she met his gaze, she could see that he understood what she'd been thinking, and she appreciated him for not teasing her.

With a small nod, she forced her insecurities out of her mind. The paddle in her hand broke the glassy surface, and the refraction of light off of the water distracted her. Long enough for a pair of hands to nudge her, and send her off-balance and plunging into the dark water around her. Jordan's yelp of surprise cut off into gurgles as she fought to suppress her laughter and hold her breath.

Once she broke the surface again, she turned her glare on the man doubled over his paddle dragging in heaving breaths. "Oh, you think this is funny, do you?" Dropping her paddle onto her board, Jordan allowed herself to sink far enough that the water danced under her eyes. She eased around to the back of her board. Chase caught her movement, and held out a hand in supplication.

"Wait, please, don't! Jay-" The resulting splash when she flipped the side of his board made the chill in her bones well worth it. When he resurfaced, she smirked at him. "Yeah, you're *so* funny."

"What is it they say about payback?" She swatted water at him with a giggle. It wasn't until fingers wrapped around her wrist that she realized her mistake, and Jordan found herself against a wall of muscle. Wide forest green eyes stared up at Chase's tanned face, and he leaned forward until his breath danced across her ear.

"You tell me," he rumbled. Before she could lean back to ask him what that meant, his hands were on her waist and his fingertips were tickling her bare skin. Jordan squealed and struggled to pull away, but his hold was strong. No matter how much she flailed, he stayed with her.

"Stop! Chase, pleasepleasestop," she begged between gasps and peals of laughter. His own amusement vibrated through her arms as she pushed against his chest, and he continued his attack until she dropped her head onto his shoulder in defeat. "Okay, I'm sorry! Uncle! You win!" Finally Chase let up and his arms locked around her back, keeping her close. His powerful legs kicked a steady rhythm, keeping them both above water as she caught her breath. The thump of his pulse under her ear soothed Jordan's own heartbeat.

Jordan realized that she hadn't felt this relaxed and *light* with someone in...*years*. Even in the best times with Adam, she hadn't been as at ease as she found herself in that moment, wrapped in Chase's arms. He loosened his grip as she leaned back, his gaze warm and filled with laughter when she looked up at him.

Before she even realized what she was doing, Jordan tugged on his shoulders to bring him to her level and pressed her lips to his. Chase made a soft noise of surprise, but responded by tightening his hold with his left arm. His right hand cradled her cheek, and she leaned into his touch. His lips tasted faintly salty from the bay water. His grip lit her nerves aflame.

He broke the kiss slowly, lingering for a moment before drawing back. Jordan pressed her forehead to his, struggling to get her pulse under control once more. As brief as the embrace had been, it left her reeling.

"Jordan, I want you to hear me," he breathed, using the hand on her cheek to tilt her head and draw her eyes back to his. He waited until she nodded to continue. "This has *nothing* to do with what I want, and *everything* to do with what you need right now. Do you understand?" Jordan nodded again, already knowing what he would say next. "If we don't wait until after everything is finished, we will have that hanging over our heads. Whether you are emotionally finished with him or not, you know there will still be guilt if you don't wait for those papers."

What they had just shared, what she was feeling, crashed into her, flaming her cheeks with embarrassment. She nodded her agreement, and did her best to turn her face away.

"Yeah...yeah you're right." Even knowing he was right didn't stop tears from burning her eyes. Why had she been so *impulsive*?

"Hey," he insisted, "I meant it when I said this has nothing to do with what I want right now. As much as I *want* to continue kissing you, if we do this, we're going to do it right. I am willing to wait. I'll be here, okay?" Jordan nodded with a shuddering breath. She turned her head and pressed her lips to his palm, and Chase kissed her forehead. He reached over and grabbed her oar from next to his own board, and held it out to her. The pair shared shy smiles when their fingers brushed, and she hauled herself back up onto the board.

Rather than standing up again, Jordan flipped onto her back and dropped an arm over her eyes. Chase chuckled at her. "What happened to showing you my favorite spot?"

The brunette lifted her arm, watching as the fireman settled into a sitting position, his legs dragging through the water. It amazed her how easily they returned to their comfortable dynamic. He grounded her in a way no one else had been able to before. "I think I want to just chill for a minute. So either lay back and work on that ridiculous tan of yours, or get outta here," she teased. Chase shook his head with a wry grin, paddled himself over to her so they were floating side by side, and hooked his bare ankle over hers to keep himself anchored to her. Jordan couldn't suppress the giddy smile, or the butterflies.

She couldn't bring herself to care that there would be a goofy tan line on her ankle when all was said and done.

***

"Wakey wakey, Davis." The voice, combined with a jolt of cold on her sun-heated skin, startled Jordan from her doze. Had she not been laying flat on her back she would have been back in the water once again.

"How nice of you." She shook off the water he'd splashed on her. "What time is it?"

"You were only asleep for a few minutes. I figured you might prefer not to be a tomato tomorrow." Jordan raised an eyebrow at him, towering over her as he stood on his board. Chase gestured behind her. "We're not far from the place I want to show you. Thankfully we didn't drift far, otherwise this little adventure could have gotten interesting. Let's go, Sleeping Beauty."

Jordan rolled her eyes playfully at him, and lifted herself up to her feet. They paddled in silence for a while, Jordan following Chase's lead. They maneuvered through the waterways among boat houses and restaurants, and then around a broad bend into a quieter area. Jordan understood right away why he'd been drawn to this place; it was quiet, undisturbed, and had a small stretch of beach to relax on should he so choose. "Wow..." she breathed.

Chase beamed over at her, and tilted his head. "You want to stop for a little while before we head back?"

Jordan looked around before turning her gaze on him. Had this happened in another month, she knew she would have said yes in a heartbeat. After what had already transpired, everything in her wanted to say yes, to spend the day alone on that beach just *being* with him; talking, learning, teaching… taking time to get to know one another without feeling as though it was wrong.

Unfortunately, it *wasn't* a month in the future, she *was* still married and it *did* feel wrong. She'd made a commitment, for better or worse; until that commitment officially ended, Jordan had made a promise to herself and to God to respect it. Spending time with Chase was one thing, but making the conscious decision to put herself in a romantic setting with him *screamed* trouble. If today had taught her anything, when it came to Chase, maintaining her resolve would be enough of a struggle as it was. "I...I don't think that's a good idea."

He nodded with affection in his eyes. "As you wish," he murmured, turning himself around and leading her back to the spot they'd dropped the boards into the water. They chatted here and there on the way in, and when they got close to shore, she used her paddle to push him off balance one last time. Before he could retaliate (or even regain his bearings from his impromptu dip), she swung herself down into the water, and pushed against the waves to get to the shore as quickly as possible. Jordan yelped when she heard him chase her. As soon as she was on shore, she deposited her board onto the beach and turned back to face Chase with her oar brandished like a staff. "You are so going to pay for...that...uh...Davis?" He carefully placed his board down, not taking his eyes from her.

"Bring it on, Falkland." Chase looked as though he was considering taking her challenge, but self-preservation must have won out as the oar fell from his hands. He shook his head, amusement sparkling in his eyes.

"I think it's my turn to call uncle on this one. I'm thinking it's about time for some ice cream?" The way Jordan's face lit up brought a grin to his lips, and he scooped up his board again. "I'll take that as a yes. Let's get these bad boys up to the car." Sand and shells crunched under their feet, serving as the only sound until they got to the street and Chase's car. As if the harbor had been its own world, stepping off of the sand brought them back into civilization where the bustle of summer beach life hit them like a crashing wave.

While Chase secured their boards, Jordan turned away and watched the tourists pass them by. In that moment, she felt incredibly peaceful. Her world was *right*.

"Adam, *no*. Stop, leave it alone." Her blood turned to ice as the all too familiar voice reached her.

Or not. "Hello, Jordan."

Chapter Nine

Every muscle in Jordan's body tightened, her instincts screaming at her to *run*. She'd made it six months without seeing the man responsible for turning her life upside down...the last thing she'd wanted was to break that streak with Chase mere feet away. She cleared her throat, calling on all of her work experience to mask any sign of discomfort. "Adam." As she turned to face him, Jordan crossed her arms tightly across her chest to hide the tremor in her hands. "Cassandra."

She resisted looking at the blonde woman, instead turning a stony gaze to her ex-husband. Cassandra, once so dear to her, cowered behind his right shoulder. Adam stood tall, arrogance rolling off of him and threatening to overwhelm

Jordan. In an instant, she felt herself reverting back to the broken, subdued girl he'd made her when she was under his thumb.

"Long time no see, eh?" he crooned, stepping closer to her. "You look great, sweetheart. Doesn't she look great, Cass?"

"Adam, that's *enough*. Let's go." Jordan's attention shifted to the woman pulling at her ex-husband's hand. The sight of their fingers intertwined rolled her stomach, and she swallowed thickly. "I'm-I'm sorry," Cassandra whispered, giving Adam's hand one last desperate pull. Jordan forced down a hollow sob, allowing only a huff of disbelief to escape her lips.

"You've lost weight," Adam continued, ignoring his companion. He disentangled their hands and stepped forward again, far too close for her comfort. "Nice to see you finally found something that worked."

Jordan felt his words like a punch to the gut, and it took everything inside of her to keep her back straight. The breath caught in her chest, and she pleaded for the strength to force back the tears threatening to make an appearance. His shadow seemed to tower over her, taunting her with the memory of every slight he'd made against her over the years. She wanted to say something back, but was too afraid her voice would crack.

An arm crossed her chest suddenly, firm hand pressing against her collarbone to ease her backwards. Instead of looking at Adam, she found herself staring at the broad, tan expanse of Chase's back. "It is time for you to move along, Davis." Chase was using every bit of his military training (and the intense workout regime that his job required) to his advantage. Jordan couldn't help the twinge of satisfaction when Adam cowered for a moment before his cool facade took over again.

Chase was *everything* Adam was not...*everything* Adam wanted to be. To her ex-husband, nothing mattered more than his appearance, but that was the one thing he could not fake. He poured countless hours into trying to become someone like Chase...running into her with a man that represented everything he couldn't reach must've been a shock to his system.

"Falkland. Maybe you should let her fight her own battles. Though, I can't say I'm surprised that it's *you* playing white knight. You were just waiting for the perfect chance to slide right in, weren't you?"

Out of Adam's direct line of sight, her fortitude waned and she started curling in on herself. She hated that he could so easily reach into her and tear apart all of the work she'd done in the months since they separated. Her forehead met the tightly-coiled muscles in Chase's back, and he took a slow, steadying breath. "This isn't a battle so much as an ambush. Walk away." If he was surprised by Cassandra's presence, he gave no indication.

"Adam, please, let's *go*," Cassandra pleaded. Jordan drew in a deep breath, and straightened to meet her eyes around Chase's shoulder. Humiliation was clear, and Jordan almost felt sorry for her. *Almost*. Adam stared up at Chase for another moment, before turning to the blonde and dropping an arm around her shoulder with exaggerated movements.

"Not worth it anyway," Adam taunted, meeting Jordan's eyes briefly to make sure she clearly understood what he meant, before turning a stiff Cassandra around and leading her away.

As soon as he was sure that they were out of earshot, Chase spun around. Jordan was staring at the couple's retreating forms, until he stepped into her line of vision. Even still, she could not completely shake herself from the shock of seeing them together. "Hey, Jordan, you're okay." Chase managed to keep his voice even, and drew her eyes up to his with a finger under her chin. "How about we get that ice cream we talked about?"

She nodded, and he wrapped his arms around her comfortingly. Jordan tucked herself under his chin, allowing herself a moment to simply feel his warmth. Even the safe feeling of his arms around her could not keep the memories away. This was certainly not the first time Adam had talked to her like that, making her feel small and broken. It amazed her though, that even after *nine months* the simple sound of his voice and a few well chosen words could bring her down so far.

***

Jordan had just finished straightening her hair when there was a soft knock on the door. She knew that Adam wouldn't have heard it, if the music from upstairs was any indication, so she bounced down the hall. Excitement thrummed through her, and she grinned widely when Danielle stepped into the townhouse.

"Hey, you look great! Kyle isn't going to know what to do with himself when he sees you!" Danielle blushed shyly and hugged Jordan. The brunette couldn't be happier for her friend; they'd met Kyle the week before through a mutual friend, and he and Danielle had both been utterly smitten from moment one. "Adam, Danny's here, let's get going babe!"

Several minutes later her husband finally made an appearance. He bounded halfway down the stairs, but stopped short when he saw Danielle. "Wow, you look effing hot, Danny!"

Jordan pushed down the pang of hurt when he then looked her over and didn't comment further. He wrapped his arms around their friend, who was watching Jordan with sympathy in her eyes. "Uh...thanks, Adam. How about Jordan? Doesn't she look fantastic too?" When he pulled back, she raised an expectant eyebrow at him.

Adam glanced between the two women, uncaring of his faux pas. "I mean, it's not like she's trying to impress someone, right? You look fine, Jordan."

Jordan turned and hurried into the kitchen to grab her purse in order to give herself a moment to force back tears. Part of her screamed at her to run upstairs and change into something better, but she couldn't bring herself to let him know just how much his words hurt her. Besides, she thought to herself, he'd just get mad at me for making him look like a jerk. She heard Danielle mutter something to him, annoyance clear in her voice, and hoped that the whole thing was forgotten by the end of the night so that it didn't turn into a fight. Plastering on a bright smile that she knew wouldn't quite reach her eyes, Jordan ignored the self-conscious doubts running through her mind and returned to the foyer, refusing to meet the eyes of either Danielle or Adam. "Ready to go?"

***

-Chase-

Chase pressed a tender kiss to the crown of her head to draw her back to the present, and then reached into his car and grabbed his shirt and her cover. They walked in silence to the ice cream shop, Jordan even subdued once she had a mint chip cone. Chase took her hand, and Jordan followed without resistance. She didn't look up until her feet hit the sand. He was rewarded with a timid smile, and they made their way to the water line before sitting down together. Sandals slid off easily, and he tossed them aside.

"So I guess this is becoming our unofficial spot, then?" she asked lightly. Chase nodded, watching her pensively while he munched on what was left of his cone. He could tell that she needed to talk, to get everything off of her chest, but he didn't want to push her. Aside from what little he'd gathered from the handful of times he'd met Adam before their split, and suspicions about Cassandra's conveniently timed disappearance from discipleship group, Jordan hadn't been keen on sharing the specifics thus far.

Based on her reaction to seeing them, though, there was a lot he didn't know.

"I'm sorry that you had to see that. If I never bumped into them again, it would have been too soon. I had somehow managed to avoid it until today; almost eight months since Adam and I were face-to-face." Jordan shook her head with a wry smile. "I do have to say, though, the timing ended up being pretty much perfect. He was freaked out by you stepping in."

"I did notice that." He tried not to sound smug.

"He is incredibly vain...so you would be unbelievably intimidating to him." Chase looked over to her. A fresh wave of protectiveness washed over him. A husband's duty was to protect his wife, and the Coast Guard core values: honor, respect, *devotion to duty*. Adam failed as a husband, and as a Guardsman, and nearly ruined a life in the process. Fortunately, Jordan leaned on her faith and came out stronger for it.

"He clearly thinks he is more intimidating than he is," he commented, raising an eyebrow at Jordan. She giggled with an enthusiastic nod. "So that's the reason that she left the group?"

The smile fell from her face. "I don't know if she ever planned on telling me. When he came back, she let it slip that she'd seen him over Christmas. He'd come back while I was visiting family, and apparently that was when it stopped being one-sided." Silence settled between them for a moment, and the pair both looked out to the ocean.

"It took a long time to forgive myself for the divorce. I'd known early on that he wasn't actually a Christian...but I kept telling myself *I* could save him. I was so desperate to lead him to God that I didn't pay attention to the red flags. I didn't realize that he was pulling me from God instead of the other way around. It wasn't until I found myself praying one night that," she hesitated for a moment. "If I wasn't meant to be married to him, that God would end it in some way that was out of my hands...that I realized just how far I'd fallen." She paused, a shaky breath drawing Chase's gaze back to her to see tears shimmering in her eyes. He reached out and slid his fingers between hers, squeezing them comfortingly. Jordan clenched her eyes shut. A single tear spilled over her lashes. "I found myself thinking that the answer to my prayer could mean that he died, or *I* did...and I was okay with that."

The base of her ice cream cone made a feeble splash in the breaking wave. Jordan dropped her forehead to her knees. "Take your time, sweetheart. I'm not going anywhere." His hand shifted to her back, rubbing comforting circles as she visibly struggled to regain control of her emotions.

"I've never told anyone about this before. I-I think it was just one of those things I kept trying to forget about, you know? I let myself focus on my anger towards them for so long that I was able to ignore my own side of it." Green eyes turned to the horizon, and she sighed. "But now...now with that *anger* pretty much gone, I can't ignore it anymore. Now, all I feel is the hurt and the guilt."

"You have nothing to feel guilty for, Jay," Chase murmured.

The sand bit into his skin as he leaned back on his elbows, and he turned his head to watch her. She bit her lip and shrugged. "I walked away from God. I allowed myself to get drawn into an emotionally abusive relationship, allowed him to destroy any semblance of self esteem I'd ever had. I walked away from important relationships, hurt my family; I might not have been responsible for my divorce, but I was responsible for getting myself there in the first place." Jordan's bottom lip started to quiver.

"I've got you, c'mere." Strong arms tugged her close. Jordan didn't even try to resist, allowing him to position her back against his chest. "You wanted to help someone that you loved. When someone does what he did to you...it's not overnight. He gained your trust, drew you away from your friends and family, and then tried to break you." Chase felt the hitch in her breath at his words, and he leaned forward to rest his chin on her left shoulder. She sank even further into his arms, and the first sniffle reached his ears. "He *tried*. Do you hear me? *Tried*. Not *succeeded*. No matter what led you to all of this, what matters is the fact that you turned to God and allowed Him to build you back up. You *survived* because you *returned to God,* and because you are an amazingly strong and caring woman."

They sat for a long moment in silence, Chase rocking her gently back and forth as she sobbed, stroking her hair and murmuring softly into her ear. Slowly, her grief waned, and she leaned her head against his.

"Oh, man...sorry for that sob fest," she huffed, shifting to rest against his broad shoulder.

Chase kissed her temple and shook his head. "You just ran into your ex and the 'other woman' for the first time in months. I'd be concerned if that *didn't* upset you."

Cold salt water splashed her toes, and she dug them into the cool, dense sand. "Why do we have to learn everything the hard way?"

"Because sometimes we are just too stubborn to trust God's plan the first time around." Jordan turned in his arms to look at him. Chase wiped the tears away from her cheeks and smiled tenderly at her. "You know better now; you learned to trust Him, and your instincts have improved from your experience. You know what you deserve now."

"I do," Jordan whispered. She held his dark gaze seriously for a long moment before speaking again. "I know that I have to do the right thing here - I have to do it the *right way* this time. Seeing them today makes it that much harder."

"Like I said earlier, I will be here. I can wait."

The look on her face was unreadable, and Chase began to worry that he'd gone too far. Just as he was getting anxious, she gave a mock scoff. "Who said I was talking about *you*?"

He raised an eyebrow before attacking her sides with ruthless fingers. Jordan squealed, struggling futilely to escape.

"I'm sorry, what was that? I don't think I heard you," he teased as she continued to squirm. He eventually stopped, listening to her breathless giggles and feeling a weight lift off of his chest. His protective nature wanted to find Adam and remind him of what it means to be a real man, but he realized that it didn't matter anymore. She'd overcome that battle, and it brought her to this very moment...with him.

"You realize this makes you the prodigal child, right?"

Any doubt that he'd started falling for her vanished when she threw her head back against his shoulder and laughed.

Chapter Ten

Jordan noticed the sirens about thirty seconds before the fire truck rolled past her house. She knew Chase was on duty that day, and felt a pang of worry; it wasn't often that the Coast Guard's fire station was called off base to respond to a crisis, so it must have been serious. She tugged her phone out of her pocket and typed out a quick message to him, knowing that he wouldn't see it until he got back but wanting to feel like she'd done *something* useful. Sammy seemed to sense her anxiety, and followed her through the house whining.

The time seemed to drag on forever as she waited for the truck to return. Every possible scenario played over and over in her mind, and she knew that no matter what, she was in trouble with this one. She'd invested too much of her heart into him, unintentional as it might have been, and the only thing that stood between them was the paperwork looming over her head. *Their heads.* She knew that whatever happened, he was right there with her. He felt the frustration as much as she did, that much she had been able to tell in their moment on the water.

She tried to keep herself busy with housework, anywhere that she would be in view of a window to the street. Nothing seemed to help though, and every time her phone dinged she jumped. When she got the fifth notification from Instagram or Facebook, she threw her phone on the couch and walked away, much to her dog's ire. The only way to stop torturing herself would be to remove the temptation to keep checking her phone.

So instead she let Sammy out, started washing dishes, and began to pray. *God, please keep them safe. I know that we should have kept our distance, but I don't know that it's even possible for me to back off emotionally anymore. I care about Chase so much, and I know that You brought him into my life for a reason. He is a good man, a good Follower, a good leader. I trust him with my heart, and I trust him with my life. Bring him out of this, and bring his brothers out of this safely. Protect everyone involved I beg of you.*

The moment she finished her prayer, a knock sounded from her front door, and Jordan nearly sobbed. She ran to open it, and found Chase standing on the other side, the top half of his uniform stripped to his tee, and the lower half covered in soot. "Oh, thank God." Without thinking, she threw her arms around his neck and pressed her face into his shoulder. The sharp scent of smoke burned her nose and left her eyes watering, but she didn't care...he was *warm* and *solid* and holding her just as tightly as she clung to him. *Thank You, Lord.* "You're okay..."

"I'm fine," he chuckled affectionately, fingers tracing soothing circles across her back. "We're all ok, no one was seriously hurt, thankfully." His reference to the rest of the team had Jordan jerking backwards, eyes darting to the street where she fully expected to see the truck waiting for him. "It's okay, Jay...I trust them, they know some of what's going on, they won't say anything." She turned skeptical eyes to him, but there was only sincerity in his face. He nudged her inside and shut the door behind him.

With a calming breath, she allowed herself to relax against his chest, comforted by the weight of his arms as they draped around her once more. "What are you *doing* here?"

Jordan could feel his smile when he rested his cheek against the crown of her head.

"I really don't think I need to answer that," he murmured. "I saw that you'd texted me after we got back in the truck, but my phone died and I left my charger at home last night. Cam dropped me off so I could let you know that I'm okay...I didn't want you to worry and we didn't think it would be a good idea for me to text you from someone else's phone for now."

Jordan squeezed her eyes shut, guilt crashing over her at the reminder of the risk he was taking by coming to see her. "Chase..."

"Like I said, I trust them."

"But what if someone who *will* say something saw you?"

"You're worth it," he insisted. The raw honesty in his tone stole her breath, and this time the tears in her eyes could not be blamed on the smoke. How long had she waited to hear those words? Was she selfish for the warmth they left in her chest? "We made sure no one was around."

"I will not be able to forgive myself if you lose your job because I'm a worrier," Jordan whispered. "You should go...get cleaned up. Your shift is almost over, right?"

"Yeah, we're pretty much done for the day after this. I'll see you at group tonight?" Jordan nodded, and Chase pressed a kiss to her forehead.

"Yeah. Go shower, you stink," she teased, pushing him towards the door.

***

"I heard the call-out for the fire that you guys responded to, sounded intense. Everyone ok?" Brian, a civilian paramedic with a station in their township, often worked similar shifts to Chase, and the two enjoyed swapping stories. Jordan glanced at Chase as she helped Alex get the kids situated for dinner, but looked away when he caught her eyes.

"Yeah...there was a kitchen fire in one of the B&B's that got out of hand quickly. A couple guests ended up going to the hospital for smoke inhalation, but that was the worst of it. The structure is pretty well destroyed...the wind was definitely fighting us today. I'm sure if it'd taken any longer to put out, we would've needed more help."

Brian nodded and then turned his attention to Jordan. "So, what is this that I hear about you running into Adam?"

Jordan heaved a heavy sigh and dropped into the open spot on her friend's couch. Chase's leg pressed against hers as she settled back, and she turned her gaze to Alex. "Yeah. After we went paddleboarding, he and Cassandra walked by, and Adam decided it was a good time to break the last nine months of virtual silence."

"How'd that go over?"

"Like a ton of freaking bricks, let me tell ya. Not that I can say I'm surprised." Frustration surged through her, and Jordan's eyes slid to the man beside her. She wasn't ready to say anything to her group, yet...they'd hardly voiced anything to *one another*. Letting it slip to them would kill any chance of them keeping it quiet. It was bad enough Chase's fire department squad knew some of what was going on.

"I've been trying to be patient. I've given him *three months* to get the paperwork into my hands. I should have turned him in way before this for fraternization with her. And then I see him out on the street after he brushes me off about the papers, and he flaunts the fact that he's dating someone that used to be my friend too? I haven't asked for a *dime* from him since I moved out, despite the fact that gets paid over $800 a month just for being married. He has no problem throwing his marriage away for someone else, but I can't even let myself *date* now that we are actually separated." A warm hand felt heavy on her back as she leaned forward and dropped her head into her hands. "I...I'm sorry. I feel like this is never ending."

"You've been fighting for months to do the right thing, to dig deeper into your faith and forgive him. Just for him to keep adding a new reason for you to *have* to forgive him; you have every right to be upset." Jordan looked up at Brian, who was watching her and Chase with an understanding look. "Are you still thinking about reporting him to his command?"

Chase's gaze on her made the hair on the back of her neck stand on end. "I've *thought* about it, yeah...but he'd be looking at formal charges for fraud, and *both* of them would be looking at adultery and fraternization. I just, I want this to be over so that I can move *on* with my life. I don't want to ruin his, I just want to take back control over my own." Jordan shook her head tiredly, and leaned back.

When she connected with the cushion of the sofa, she realized that Chase's arm had come around her shoulders. Instinct curled her body towards him, and the ease of the movement nearly stole her breath away. "It's picking a scab open any time something happens. I get anxious every time my phone goes off, because *what if it's him*? What's the next rug he's going to rip out from under my feet, or how's he going to gaslight me this time? I just want it to be done so I can lick my wounds and actually let them heal."

"You know we're here for you always. It sounds like there's not a whole lot you can do at this point but wait, but you've got us when you feel like dealing with it alone is too much." Alex smiled at her, and Jordan could easily read the gleam in her best friend's eye. She was so going to hear about this new level of comfort with Chase as soon as they were alone.

The man in question squeezed her arm comfortingly, and she leaned her head back onto his bicep. Maybe it wouldn't have been so difficult to deal with Adam dragging his feet if it weren't for Chase. Maybe she wouldn't feel this undeniable sense of urgency. But even with the frustration, she wouldn't trade it for the peace she felt in Chase's presence.

Brian shifted the group focus to the sermon from the day before, and Jordan finally began to relax. With the attention off of her, the emotional rollercoaster of just the last *five minutes* settled into her bones. She wondered if this exhaustion would ever go away - if she'd stop yo-yoing between righteous fury and overwhelming grief every two seconds. Her heart couldn't decide how to feel at any given moment. She wanted to just *feel* one thing at a time...to *get* angry and *stay* angry until she was ready to not be anymore.

Chase's presence never wavered throughout the meeting, comforting and warm. His voice whispering her name, breath dancing across her ear, stirred Jordan, and alerted her to the fact that it was suddenly much quieter than she remembered. "Chase?" she murmured blearily.

"You fell asleep, Jay," he replied. Jordan twisted around to see an affectionate smile directed at her. A cursory glance around the room revealed that they were alone, and it was much darker than when she was last awake. "They're getting the kids ready for bed, they'll be back in a minute. Everyone else went home, said to tell you goodnight." Jordan groaned and buried her face in his shoulder. Chase's amusement rumbled through her. "Do you want me to drive you home?"

"No, I'll be fine to drive in a few minutes. You should've woken me up!"

"Jordan, you clearly needed the sleep. Besides," his voice dropped to a low tone, and he leaned in to her ear, "I've got to take advantage of the moments I can get for now." Jordan squeezed her eyes shut with a deep inhale, and then forced the air out in a huff. He helped her up, and watched her silently as she wandered around the living room to gather her things. "How do you end up with stuff all over the place? You were awake for like two hours…"

"Shut it, Falkland. I blame the runts," Jordan growled playfully, tossing a small stuffed animal at him. Chase chuckled and caught the toy with ease. Both turned to glance at Alex as she entered the room, daughter propped naturally on her hip. Jordan snuck a side glance at Chase. Her heart melted at the tender look in his eyes as he watched the little girl.

"Welcome back, Sleeping Beauty," Alex teased lightly. Jordan rolled her eyes.

"You know, any one of you could have woken me up. I'm half afraid to look at myself in the mirror, you probably drew all over my face or something." Her best friend raised an eyebrow at her, glancing at Chase as if to say *yeah, as if he'd let us near you.* In that one glance Jordan could tell she was *totally* in for an interrogation when they had dinner the next night. "Okay, I'm gonna get out of here. Goodnight, guys. Bye bye, beautiful," she cooed at Amelia, half asleep in her mother's arms. "Alex, I'll be here to get you by six!"

"Wait up, I'll walk you out!" Chase called before she could leave. Jordan sighed lightly. He was *not* making it easy to keep him within the 'friendzone'. She heard him say his goodbyes to their friends as she stepped back from the door, allowing it to close gently.

"You just can't let me make a smooth exit, can you?" she asked when he joined her.

"You call *that* smooth?" Chase teased. "You in a hurry or something?"

The cool night air brushed through her hair, and Jordan tucked a stray strand back behind her ear. "Not exactly," she murmured, abruptly solemn. "I just..I'm trying so hard to do the right thing, but it seems like every time I'm around you, it gets more and more difficult. Falling asleep on your shoulder, that felt *right*. But that's not something I'd have done with a guy friend. That's something that I'd do with a *boyfriend*. I can't keep up this distance, but we both know that forgetting about it will follow us around like a ghost. I don't know what to do, Chase."

As she finished talking, they reached her car. Jordan leaned back against her door, and Chase stepped up in front of her. Were this a *normal* situation for a *normal* couple, she would feel no shame in tugging him against her and kissing him with everything she had. Every fiber of her being was *screaming* at her to do so.

But then Chase took a step back, understanding and a touch of guilt in his eyes. "I'm sorry. That's partly my fault...I'm *sorry*. I haven't made this easy for you. But I don't want to cause you pain. You tell me what you need me to do, and I'll do it. I can completely back off until this is all over, I can ease up. What do you need?"

Jordan gazed at him for a long moment, taking in the sincerity written in the lines of his face. She knew being around him and not being *near* him would be even worse than resisting this temptation, so she curled her fingers in his shirt and tugged him forward. The Coastie gave a surprised 'oof' when their bodies collided, and she felt Chase brace himself against the roof of her car for an instant, before his arms circled her waist and hugged her. "I'll take that to mean you *don't* want me to back off?" Jordan giggled. Her face was buried against his chest, and she rocked it back and forth firmly. His responding laughter vibrated against her cheek. "Okay, okay. I won't change anything, then?"

"Please don't. I'm going to need you; I have a feeling this is gonna get uglier before it's over. The only reason I was able to get through seeing him yesterday was because you were there with me. I'm going to be reaching out to him again this week about the papers, and I know it's not going to go over well."

Hands gently eased her back so that he could draw her gaze. "I'll be here, just say the word. If he tries anything…"

"No." Jordan shook her head. "I don't think he's going to do anything like that. He's too much of a coward and has too much to lose to actually try anything. But I know how cruel he can be. With this much at stake, I'm preparing myself for worse. Worse is going to suck."

Chase's jaw clenched at that, and she nearly regretted letting that bit of information slip. She knew that he would be protective of her, and even hinting to the fact that Adam could be awful when he wanted to be would just make that more intense. "I don't know how a man justifies bringing a woman harm," he growled, "physical or mental."

"Hey, I've gotten through this much. I'll be just fine," she murmured. He pulled her close again. His chin rested on the top of her head and his warmth enveloped her.

"Still. He would be better off not seeing me if he hurts you again. Kinda difficult considering we work at the same base." They stayed that way for a while, just sharing comfort, until Jordan pushed against his chest gently. "Yeah, yeah, time to go home. Text me and let me know you got there safely, okay?"

"You are such a worrier," Jordan teased lightly, unlocking her car and watching him walk towards his own slowly. "Will do," she promised. "Goodnight, Chase."

"Goodnight, Jaybird." He didn't get into his car until she'd settled herself behind her own wheel, and then she watched silently as he reluctantly pulled away. Jordan dropped her head onto the steering wheel with a long groan, praying for time to hurry up and pass so that this torture could end.

The sudden buzzing of her phone startled Jordan, who yelped. When she checked it, Alex's name popped up: You got some 'splainin to do young lady!

Yes mother. I'll see you tomorrow.

Chapter Eleven

While she waited patiently in the driveway for her best friend, Jordan checked her texts, and sighed when there was no notification waiting for her. 'Hey, Dani, trying again in case my last message didn't go through. Want to grab some lunch sometime next week?' The phone clattered into the cupholder, and her stomach sank with dread; it was much more likely that she was being ignored, and the thought of losing Danielle, too, hurt.

"Okay, woman, you better start talking," Alex insisted the moment she got into the car. Jordan shook her head with a wry grin and pulled out of the driveway smoothly. "Are you okay?" she asked when she noticed Jordan's face.

"Just…really hate this whole divorce situation, that's all. I'm fine! Can we decide where to go first?"

"Danny's, duh. Now *spill*." The stern tone of her best friend's voice made Jordan chuckle.

"Okay, okay. We, uh…we went paddleboarding together. That's why we were together when I ran into Adam and Cassandra." The brunette braced for the impending smack on the arm, and was not disappointed. "Driving here! I know, I'm a terrible friend for not telling you. And I'm *sorry*, okay? But I-I felt guilty about it, and didn't want to say anything to *anyone*! It was bad enough you knew we were together when we saw Adam."

"Guilty, huh?"

"Of course I felt guilty. I kissed him." Red lit up her cheeks when her best friend squealed in shock.

"How dare you not call me to tell me this?! I am your *best friend*!! You *tell* me when you kiss the guy of your dreams! Why in the *world* would you feel guilty about that?"

"Because I'm still married! I can't get involved with him while I'm still legally with Adam!"

Alex sobered quickly. "Jor, you have no reason to feel guilty for what you know is between the two of you. Wait to date him, absolutely. But don't feel guilty for a moment of weakness with a man like *Chase Falkland.* He is a good man. He is a Christian...and he genuinely cares about you. He is the kind of man you should be trusting, he is the kind of man that will be a good husband. I'm not saying jump to that conclusion by any means. Too soon. But don't push him away because of a piece of paper."

"I'm not," Jordan promised with an affectionate smile over to her friend. "We are putting it on hold...well, more or less. We've talked about the feelings, we've talked about the roadblock...we're on the same page. I thought I might be able to keep him at arm's length until this is over, but *clearly*, I was wrong."

"Considering you used him as a body pillow last night? Yeah, I'd say you were wrong." Alex didn't quite manage to hide her grin. "So back to the outing. When, where, how did you get to the kissing?!"

The car came to a stop in front of a familiar restaurant, and Jordan was almost afraid to talk about it in public. She couldn't imagine putting Chase's career at risk because she admitted to being involved with him in any way where someone like Adam could hear her. "We went out after church, he showed me a place he likes to go. I was giving him a hard time when we first got out on the water, he knocked me off my board. I returned the favor...we fooled around a bit...I couldn't help but kiss him."

"Mmmmm...I'll bet it was nice, huh?"

Jordan huffed a laugh. She took advantage of the distraction of closing her door and walking into the restaurant to force her thoughts away from that moment in the water with Chase. Of course it was nice. "I...I was so overwhelmed by the fact that I was kissing him, it was over before I even realized I'd done it." Alex gave a low groan of commiseration, and Jordan grinned. The two got settled into their usual booth. "Yeah...and then the fire happened today. I saw the truck go out, and got nervous, so I texted him. He saw it, and then his phone died, so one of the guys on his crew dropped him off on the way back to the station so he could tell me that he was safe."

Alex gaped at her, imitating a fish in her shock. Jordan chuckled and shrugged, and Alex shook her head. "Wow...okay. Yeah. That's...that's something. But for now, we are *not* going to focus on him anymore, because it is not helping your situation right now, so...tell me about something else." They both giggled, and fell into easy, *safe* conversation. Jordan grinned across the table at her best friend, grateful for the ability to let go of the anxiety over her budding relationship and failing marriage and friendships, and just be with the person who knew her best in the world.

***

'I haven't asked you for much in this whole mess. But enough is enough, we need to get this over with. Do you have the papers yet?'

Stress knotted Jordan's stomach, leaving her nauseous and shaky. *Will this feeling ever go away? Will I ever be free of this?* She struggled to remember the happy times in her marriage, in her relationship with Adam at all. She knew they existed; she wouldn't have married him if she didn't have some kind of happy experience to make her fall in love.

The problem was, now that she knew more about what made him tick, every single happy memory was tainted with the shadow of *what was his motivation for doing this?* Every time she remembered something nice he did, it was overrun by doubt. How often did he do something nice just to keep her placated? How many times did he say that he'd done something, say that he *would* do something, just to shut her up? It was impossible to see in the moment, but in hindsight, she couldn't fathom how she'd gotten through it and kept her sanity. He'd played her so well. "He deserves a friggin' Oscar," she muttered to herself.

Jordan dropped back onto her bed, wishing she didn't care about the answer. Wishing she could be stronger and ignore the fact that he wasn't going to respond right away, on purpose, to keep her on her toes like he'd been so keen to do in the past. "Soon. Soon, this will be over, and if he ever texts you again, you can just delete it and know that your life is so much better without him. Oh, God...maybe I *did* lose my sanity."

She was startled, however, when her phone buzzed only a few minutes later.

'Have you seen the new superhero movie?'

What? Superhero movie?! 'No...'

'Do you want to?'

Realization dawned on Jordan. Fury was quick on its heels, and she could hear the force of her taps as she typed a response. 'Eventually, I guess. Not with you.'

A long moment passed before her phone dinged again. 'Come on, I'm trying here.'

'Trying what exactly, Adam? You were proud to flaunt Cassandra two days ago. Why aren't you asking her to go to the movies with you?' Tears of rage burned in her eyes. How *dare* he play this game after all this time?

And yet...why should she be surprised? He was the *master* of games just like this. He knew that she would feel obligated to say yes...to do what was *right*. No matter how much everything pointed to this just being another game, he knew she would allow him to try.

Instead of buzzing to notify her of a new text message, Jordan's phone started ringing. A numb sort of shock passed over her, and Jordan shook her head as she picked the device up from the table. "Adam." She couldn't believe that this was actually happening.

"Look, Jordan...Cassandra's over. I-I made amends with God and it's over. Will you go to the stupid movie with me or not?" The sound of his voice made her skin want to crawl, and all she could hear in his words were *lies...lies...lies.*

"Making amends implies that you had a relationship to begin with. Which you and I both know you did not. What exactly happened to make you see the light so quickly?"

"Look, I'm trying to do the right thing here, okay? I'm trying to fix it. Stop making this so difficult."

Jordan nearly dropped the phone, though she couldn't tell anymore if it was surprise or anger. "Ex*cuse* me?!" A silent prayer of thanks was sent for the fact that her voice didn't tremble like the rest of her body. She leapt to her feet and began pacing around her house.

"I. Am. Trying. To. Fix. This."

"And you expect me to get that out of 'have you seen the new superhero movie'? How exactly do you expect to fix anything by watching a movie, Adam?"

The growl of frustration on the other end of the line made her want to hang up and throw her phone across the room. "What would you suggest, Jordan?"

"You want so badly to fix what you messed up? You'd better *prove* it. You have *so* far to go to make me believe that you *actually* want to fix this. You need to meet me at Starbucks in Avalon tomorrow night."

"Starbucks? Really? No. If we're not going to go to a movie, then we're going to go somewhere that we can relax, have a couple of drinks and have some dinner, and really talk."

Jordan scoffed. If it weren't for her faith, she'd have hung up on him long ago. Nothing had changed with him. Nothing. "No. We are not going on a *date*. We are going to *meet* to *talk*.

This is *not* a date. Period. You are starting from less than scratch, do you understand me? You have to prove to me that I can trust you to even be my *friend* before I am going to give you the chance to prove to me that you can be my *husband* again."

The long-suffering sigh sent off warning bells in her head, and she knew in the depths of her soul that this would not be going very far. He was still the exact same man, playing games to get what he wanted. Still, though, she'd made a vow that she took very seriously, even if Adam didn't. She would do what she could to try to make it right. She *had* to. She was *obligated* to.

The thought of giving in to this made her sick to her stomach...the thought of telling Chase made her breath catch in her chest, and she nearly couldn't respond when Adam agreed to meet her the following night. The response that she *did* give was short and stern, and she hung up without giving him much chance to say anything else.

Chase...oh, Lord...Chase would never forgive her. Finally free from the need to be strong talking to Adam, Jordan sagged back down onto her bed, and released the pent up agony. Sobs racked her body as she realized what had just transpired, and what that meant for the already-fragile relationship she had with the man that was *everything* that Adam wasn't.

It took three re-writes to text Chase and ask him to meet her at their 'spot' after he got off work. Sammy whined at her feet, and Jordan ran her shaking fingers through the thick fur. "I don't know if I can do this, Sammy. I can't hurt him. I can't ruin this when I know that Adam hasn't changed. But...but if I don't...if I don't I'll always feel that guilt just like if I started a relationship with Chase. I don't know what to do."

She decided to go to the lighthouse early and spend some time with God before Chase arrived. She was going to need all of the strength she could get to do what needed to be done. And if He so chose to tell her otherwise, far be it for her to deny Him the chance. She quickly texted Alexandra to update her on the situation, and wasn't surprised when her best friend called her seconds later.

"Please tell me you're joking right now?" Alex demanded. Jordan's silence spoke for her. "Oh, Jordan." Alex heaved a resigned sigh. "What are you going to tell Chase?"

"I'm going to tell him the truth; it's all I can do. I hate Adam for doing this to me when I *know* that he's not changed. But I have to do the right thing and at least hear him out."

"Doesn't mean we have to like it," Alex muttered. Jordan chuckled and agreed wryly. "And let me tell you, if he pulls something and hurts you again, I'll kill him."

"Oh hush, you. I love you for being protective, but it'll be okay. I'm expecting the worst from him, so I'll be fine. It's Chase that we need to worry about. He's never going to forgive me."

"No, Jor. He'll forgive you no matter what. He's a good man...that's what they do. He won't abandon you. You just need to be prepared to give him some time, you know?"

"Yeah...yeah, I know. One of the many things I adore about him."

***

Please, Father, help me to find the strength to tell Chase the truth. Give him peace, help him to understand that I have to do this. Help me understand why I have to do this. Why, when things are starting to seem so much better, did this have to happen? Is this a test, or something? To figure out how much I am willing to give up to be obedient to You? I can't put myself back into a situation where Adam has the power to hurt me again...but I know You can work miracles. So if this is for real, I am going to do the right thing. I will stand by my husband. But please, God, if it's not real, if this is just another game for him, please show me clearly. I don't want to wonder if I am doing the right thing, either way. Make the right choice abundantly clear to me, I beg of you.

"Okay, Davis, what's got you worked up?"

Chase's voice jolted her from her prayer and triggered the sting of tears in her eyes, and she fought to hold them back as he dropped down beside her. The brush of his shoulder against hers lit her nerve endings on fire, and it took all of her willpower not to lean away from him. If this was the last time they were this close, she was going to draw as much strength and comfort from it as she could. "How do you know I'm worked up?" The waver in her voice had Jordan cringing instantly.

Chase's raised eyebrow as he turned his head to look at her dashed any hopes he hadn't heard it too. "You mean besides the fact that you're trying to hide your crying from me? Your text was just, off." His eyes darted between hers like he was trying to read her without her having to tell him. "What's going on, Jay?"

She took a deep breath, steeling herself for the words she desperately wanted to keep locked inside of her head, and chewed anxiously on her bottom lip. " I, I, uh…I finally got an answer about the papers from Adam." Chase's shoulders and jaw tensed, instantly alert, but he allowed her to continue. She could feel the weight of his gaze, but couldn't find the strength to meet it with her own. "He...he told me he wants to fix it."

His sharp inhale felt like a suckerpunch, and the first of her tears spilled over onto her cheek. "F-fix it?" Jordan opened her mouth to speak, but could only nod when no sound would come out. "We just saw him three days ago with the woman he *left* you for. That's a hell of a turnaround," he growled. Jordan tucked her knees up to her chest and wrapped her arms around them in an attempt to ease the rolling in her stomach and the tremors in her hands. "Jordan, you and I both *know* that this is another one of his sick games." His voice was even, but there was a biting edge to his tone.

"I know," Jordan whispered, sniffling quietly and trying to brush the evidence of tears away. "Believe me, I *know* that. I'm sure this is just a twisted ploy to turn this around somehow on me. But you also know that I *have* to do this the right way. I *have* to give him that chance. Who am I to tell God that He hasn't whacked Adam over the head in the last three days, and made him see the light?"

"And if He hasn't? What then, are you going to subject yourself to that asshole's abuse again? Did you already forget how powerless he made you feel?" It hurt her to know that she was the reason behind the edge she'd never heard before in his voice. She had to fight the instinct to recoil like she'd done so many times before when Adam would lash out at her. *He's not going to hurt me, he's not mad* at *me.*

"Of course not." She finally looked up at him, and couldn't hold back the fresh tears when she saw the raw hurt and rejection in his eyes. "I know better now. I can read through his lies...I *know* what a real marriage looks like. *You taught me* what a good man looks like. I won't fall for it again. Chase, I *have to do this,*" she pleaded, praying that he would understand how much this tore her apart. "The *last* thing I want to do is go back to him, but it is my duty as a wife to at least try."

"Why do *you* have to be the one to take the higher road?" Chase muttered, turning his head to stare out over the ocean. With that question, Jordan knew that he understood. It didn't take away the pain for him, but he was letting her know that he didn't *hate* her. Whether he'd ever be able to look at her again? That was a different story.

"For the same reason nothing happened between us so far. I'm sorry, Chase; this hurts me too, you know that. I feel like you were brought into my life for a reason. That it isn't over yet. The thought of even giving a chance for him to get in the way of that, I...I just..."

"You don't need to explain yourself, Jordan. I get it, I do. Just...you told me that when you prayed for a sign regarding your marriage, you did so thinking that if it needed to, it could end by one of you *dying*. He'd put you in such a bad place that you were okay if death was your escape from him. You asked for a sign, and your husband asked for a divorce. Maybe you were already given your answer." He ran a hand through his hair and took a shaky breath. "I understand that you need to see this through. I just...I need some time." Without waiting for her to respond, Chase pushed himself up to his feet. "Just don't forget to listen to God's voice in all of this, and don't lose yourself, okay? Don't forget what you're worth."

"Chase...*Chase!*" The fireman ignored her calls, kicking up sand in his determination to get away from her. "I'm sorry," she whimpered, pressing her forehead to her knees and finally allowing her sobs loose. Tears soaked her shirt, but she couldn't bring herself to try to wipe them away. The best thing that God had brought into her life since she got to the Cape had just walked away from her, and she had no idea if he'd ever accept her again.

By the time her tears subsided, the sun had set. For the first time, watching the rainbow of colors float over the water did nothing to calm her; her peace was shattered, and it felt as though it would never return. "God, I'm begging you to help me. I don't think I can take going back to the life I had with Adam…I can't let him treat me like nothing again. I know that You love me. I know that I am worth the love of a *good man* because of You, and my instincts are telling me that he has not changed.

"If I have to go through with this, You are going to have to carry me every single day because I can't do it on my own. I can't look at Adam knowing that Chase wants to be with me. And even though Adam has wronged me, he should have a wife that is devoted to him. I don't know if I can be that for him after what I know now, and I know that it is not how a Godly wife *should* be. I am sorry, God, for faltering in my patience. I'm sorry for allowing Chase into my heart before my marriage was over. Please don't punish Chase for my mistake."

She left the beach feeling no lighter than she'd come in; the weight of her fear and turmoil sat heavily on her shoulders.

Chapter Twelve

The door of the coffee shop dinged merrily in a stark contrast to the emotions of the young woman walking through it. Jordan looked down at her hand as she released the handle, and groaned inwardly at how visibly it was shaking. She didn't want to show Adam any sign of weakness; he was expecting her to be the same scared little girl he'd left behind...the little girl he'd brought out in her just days before. She was determined not to allow herself to become that scared again; now, she was going to show him just who she'd become *without* him. If he'd truly changed, he would appreciate her strength. If he hadn't, he would be threatened by it, and he would try to bring her back down, try to assert his control over her once more.

"Hey there, what can I get for you?" The barista smiled sympathetically at her, as if she could sense Jordan's anxiety. The brunette stared at the menu for a moment, realizing quickly that no matter what she bought, she would feel too nauseous to drink anything.

"Uh...can I just get a vanilla chai, medium please?" She paid for her order and sat silently, making sure she was facing the door so that she could be prepared when he showed up. She pulled out her phone, checking the time. Adam should be arriving any time.

Her drink came and she sipped numbly at it, barely even noticing the burn on her tongue. Every time someone walked by the door, she tensed, and every time someone entered, she had to take another drink to occupy her fidgeting fingers. A dull throb had started in her left temple, and frustration slowly started to seep into her bones. With another check to her phone, Jordan noted that fifteen minutes had passed. She was mildly impressed that it had already been fifteen minutes, considering how slowly time usually passed when she was anxious.

"Why am I not surprised?" she muttered to herself as she pulled up his contact to call him. The ringing of Adam's phone made her skin crawl, and she hung up before the voicemail message had time to play through completely.

Jordan sat like that for another thirty minutes: alone, waiting for her soon-to-be ex husband and feeling like an idiot for falling for it. She texted Adam, and then called him once more. This time she left him a voicemail, telling him that he'd made a pretty big mistake in trying to prove himself to her. She finally tossed her tea into the trash, shrugged to the barista, and stomped her way back to her car. Fury radiated through her, making all of her movements exaggerated. She had to admit to herself, though, that slamming her car door did feel a smidge satisfying.

Halfway home, her cell phone started ringing, and Jordan could have screamed. Adam's name blinked across her dash screen. Jordan gave it a few seconds before answering. "So, did you forget something?"

"*Uh...yeah, I'm sorry about that. I got held up late at work.*"

"So you can text all day when it suits you, but you can't be bothered to tell me that you were late *before* I waited for almost an hour?"

"*Don't be like that, Jordy. My phone was dead,*" Adam cooed. Jordan had to fight to suppress her growl.

"Oh, that's funny, because it rang through every single time, Adam. That story isn't going to fly anymore."

"Ok fine, I'm done now, I can meet you there. I'll be there in ten minutes."

Jordan barked a bitter laugh. "You blew your chance today. If you want to meet, you need to give me a few days so that I can calm down. It took me a lot to give you a chance today, so you'll forgive me if I'm a little upset right now."

"A few days? What are you talking about? No way. Meet me there in ten minutes," Adam commanded. Jordan was taken aback, though she wasn't sure if it was by him or by her own naivety before he left her. Either way, she knew she wasn't going to let him walk all over her anymore. It was time for her to stand up for herself.

"Absolutely not. You are not in control here anymore. Adam, *you* were the one who screwed up. *You* were the one who fell in love with another woman, and *you* were the one walking hand in hand with said woman four days ago. If I tell you I need a few days to cool down so that I don't say something that I regret when I see you, you are going to give me a few days to cool down. You tell me that you found God. You spent almost a year without me. A few more days won't hurt you. It would even be a good time to spend in prayer over how to be respectful to your wife."

Adam was silent for a long moment. Jordan had just started wondering if he'd hung up when he finally exhaled, and she rolled her eyes at his words. *"You are holding on to your anger, you know. And you're only hurting yourself here. I don't need you in my life, I'm doing the* right thing." Jordan sent a silent prayer to God for the strength to hold her tongue, and shook her head.

"I am not holding on to my anger. I have every right to be upset right now. *You stood me up.* I gave you the chance to prove that you've changed, and guess what, Adam? You failed that test. If you leave me alone for three days, then I will give you *one final chance.*"

"I failed? I failed?! You are the one who is unwilling to compromise at all here, Jordan! And don't even use Cassandra as an excuse, because if I recall correctly, you weren't alone either! How's Falkland doing, anyway?"

Jordan had to pull into a small shop parking lot. She squeezed her eyes shut tightly, and took several deep breaths. "He is my *friend*, Adam. Nothing more. Unlike you, I am able to respect the fact that I am *still legally married*. Or did you forget that you never got those papers to me like you were supposed to three months ago?"

The image of Adam's face turning beet red almost brought a smile to her face in spite of her anger. His breathing sped up, and she knew he was struggling to understand why she was talking back to him. "You *are responsible for this marriage falling apart now, Jordan. I tried to make this right, but you're the one who can't be flexible and forgive a simple mistake.*"

"You know what, Adam? I recognize that you can't see past your own agenda here, so if that's what you need to tell yourself in order to be okay with this, fine. But my asking for three days to separate myself from my hurt and anger about what just happened is *not* unreasonable. I know that you don't understand what's happening right now, because this is nothing like how I'd have responded to you a year ago. But I'm not that girl anymore, the one who would've done anything to appease you. I found myself when you left, Adam. I will not grovel and sacrifice who I am to make *you* feel better about yourself."

"*Oh get off your high horse, Jordan.*" His voice was full of irritation and Jordan could clearly imagine the expression on his face. Her stomach knotted just from the image of his annoyance.

"You just can't accept responsibility for what you're doing. You've changed, and I don't like this angry person that you've become."

"Goodbye, Adam."

As soon as she hung up, she tossed the phone to her passenger seat, and rested her forehead on her steering wheel. *It's over. It's really over. He truly hasn't changed, and I'm done letting him hurt me. It. Is. Over. Thank you, God!*

Jordan took several deep, calming breaths, and couldn't help but smile. The terrible weight that had been sitting on her chest since the first text message finally lifted. She'd done what she needed to do: gave Adam the chance to prove himself when telling her that he'd changed. He'd failed that particular test miserably, and she finally felt free from his reach. Any remaining question in her mind had been banished.

She scrambled blindly for her phone for a moment, the lingering adrenaline from her argument with Adam leaving her feeling shaky. 'Lex...it's over. He stood me up.'

Before she could make the phone call she desperately wanted to make, Jordan put her car into drive, and got back out on the street. She needed to get to her quiet space before she called Chase. She wanted to be calm, steady when she spoke to him again.

The beach was blessedly empty when she arrived, and the steady breeze coming from the water made her feel alive. Staring out across the vast blue expanse before her, she finally pulled out her phone and selected Chase's number from her contact list. Each ring disheartened her a little more, and she realized that it was probably too soon for him. He needed space; he was hurt by what she'd told him, and it would take time for him to be ready to talk to her again. "Hey, Chase, it's me. I-I just...I need to talk to you. It's too much to tell your voicemail. I'm so, *so* sorry Chase. I never wanted to hurt you in all of this. Please call me back."

The brunette dropped the phone to her side, her excitement dissipating. Even so, the relief from the definitive answer from Adam radiated through her, giving her hope to move on from the nightmare that had been her marriage.

Chapter Thirteen

"The Kline boys are on their way! And that closes out the PreK Class." Jordan held out her hands as the two young boys bounced towards the door, and couldn't suppress the grin as they jumped to give her a high-five before darting out to the church foyer to meet their parents. Jordan turned to Alexandra and pulled her name lanyard over her head. "That was an awesome Sunday school!"

"Yeah it was! Thank you, Jordan. Now get outta here, I know you have someone to try to catch," her best friend said with a knowing look. Jordan gave her a grateful smile, and jogged out to the main sanctuary. A quick sweep allowed her to locate Chase, just walking out of the building.

"Chase!" she called, pushing to reach him before he got into his car. Jordan stopped in the doorway. "Chase, wait up!" The Coastie barely turned back with a firm shake of his head, before opening his door and sliding in. The rejection stung, and tears burned in her eyes, but she couldn't blame him for avoiding her.

"Jordan..."

The woman in question felt her breath catch in her throat. The tears threatening to fall made her throat feel dry and constricted, but Jordan forced back her emotions behind a blank mask and turned around to face Cassandra. "What are you doing here?" she growled in a low tone. Cassandra looked meek and afraid, but Jordan couldn't bring herself to feel bad for the woman.

"I'm here to say goodbye. And I'm sorry."

Jordan scoffed and grabbed her by the wrist. Cassandra didn't resist as Jordan pulled her away from the building. "You're *sorry*? Now? After what happened last week, *now* you are sorry?"

"Look, I think you know a little about how good Adam is at ensnaring you in his trap. He's very good at making everything seem okay, no matter how much you think it's wrong. There were a lot of things that he told me about your relationship that I didn't question until we saw you that day. I know I hurt you...I've always known that. And I've always been sorry for that. But seeing you while I was with him, I just...it changed everything. I wanted to let you know that I ended things with Adam."

Jordan tilted her head in curiosity, confusion clear in her eyes. "*You* ended things?"

"Yeah. After the way he treated you when we ran into you, I realized that he'd been putting on a show. That he really was as selfish underneath all of it as I'd known deep down all along." She sighed heavily, dropping her gaze to the floor. "I requested a transfer to Sitka. I'm leaving at the end of the week."

Jordan stared at Cassandra in shock, and for the first time understood that, in part, she'd been a victim as well. While her behavior was wrong, and she *had* betrayed a dear friend, Adam was the one at the root of it all. *He* was the one lying and manipulating both of them. And yet, she still found herself unable to let go of the hurt and disconnection from her former friend. "Thank you for telling me. Have a safe trip, Cassandra."

The petite blonde gave her a timid, watery half-smile, and walked away. Jordan released a shaky breath and made her way silently towards her car. Apparently today was just not her day to connect with anyone. "I need to spend some time with God, anyway," she murmured to herself as she climbed into her car.

***

The following day found Jordan busy at work, searching through desk drawers and in random cabinets.

"Hey, Alex, have you seen the scissors? I've got a tag that Fiona wants to get rid of, but the scissors aren't in their usual cabinet," Jordan called to her best friend. She looked over to see Alex pulling a lunch tray off of the nearest cafeteria table. Alex simply shook her head and went on with her task.

Jordan turned to her patient waiting expectantly, and shrugged. "Sorry, Fi, I'll see if I can find another pair somewhere and let you know, okay?"

"Aw, okay. Thanks, Jordy." She watched her patient trudge away to get her lunch with an affectionate smile.·

"Oh, hey, Jordan!" David called from the next room. Jordan looked over to her coworker, walking his way when he waved her over. "You looking for scissors? I put them on the desk in the rec room office."

Alarm sparked in her chest. "I'm sorry, you left them *where*?"

David looked dumbfounded at her concern, and looked around. "Uh...the...rec room office?" She closed her eyes and dragged in several slow breaths to calm herself down. "Was that wrong?"

Jordan bit her lip to keep herself from lashing out at him. "Look, David, I know you're new here, but you have *got* to have common sense when it comes to safety. What kind of ward do we work in?"

"A psychiatric ward?"

"Yes. And what office do the patients - some of whom have violent paranoid delusions - have access to during down time, like right now?"

Horror finally dawned in his eyes, and the color drained from David's face. "The...rec room office..."

Jordan nodded angrily and pointed towards the rec room. "You need to go and make sure they are still in there. Now."

Before he could move, a shout of alarm rang out from the cafeteria. Both staff members immediately darted in the direction of the sound, and saw three patients locked in a tussle. "All patients need to go *back to your rooms. Now!*" Several complied immediately, unwilling to be caught up in the chaos of a fight. She nodded over to Alex, who sidestepped around the fight and hit the panic alarm.

The wailing deterred most of the remaining patients, scattering them to the various wings as other doors locked down. Jordan carefully stepped closer to the fight, looking for an opening to get through to one of the men. David stepped forward too, but looked as though he was ready to try to pull one of them away. "Back off, David. Don't try to play hero right now, just give them a minute," she growled. The new employee glanced at her, but did not listen. As he reached for the nearest swinging patient, Jordan stepped around to block his route. David scrambled to a stop, and she stared him down. "I. Said. Back. Off. You-"

"Jordan!" Alex cried in panic. A thick arm wrapped around Jordan's throat, cutting off her air. "Michael," Alex's voice took on a soothing calm. "You need to let her go. She is trying to help you, okay? Just let her go."

"Make him...make him go away," the patient stuttered, gesturing with his free hand at David. Jordan's eyes locked on the flash of metal in his hands. *The missing scissors. Perfect.* Alex gestured firmly for him to remove himself from the situation.

Jordan's hands grasped Michael's arm desperately, pulling despite knowing that he was much stronger than she was. *Please, God...get us out of this alive.*

"Okay...okay, Michael, David's gone. Can you tell me why you are hurting Jordy right now?" The nickname would hopefully help ground the man in reality and remind him that she was a friend.

"You all want to-want to hurt us! We were fighting, *shouldn't* have been fighting. He said he was going to hurt me if I didn't give him the scissors." When Michael used the scissors to point to another man he'd been fighting, his eyes were drawn to a door at the far end of the room. Three guards stood, guns aimed and ready, prepared to move the instant he showed any weakness. "No! No, don't hurt me! They're going to hurt me! Jordy is one of *them*, she wants to hurt me too!"

Jordan tried desperately to shake her head, but her attention was fading out as darkness started to invade her vision. "M-Mi..."

Her abdomen tensed abruptly when the cold sharp point of the scissors dug into her side. "Shut up! Get away from me! I...I'll kill her! Get away!"

"Michael, *please*...she's always been there to help you, remember? She's always been the one to get you that extra snack, she's the one that always plays cards with you. You don't want to hurt her, Michael. She is your friend," Alex soothed. Jordan could read the panic in her eyes, and felt a swell of pride at the steadiness of her best friend's voice.

"Michael, you need to put the scissors down *right now!* I don't want to have to hurt you, but I can't let you hurt her." Christopher, one of the security guards, stepped further into the room, drawing Michael's attention once more. A sharp jolt of pain drew a cry from Jordan, and Christopher stopped moving. "Okay, okay, I'll stay right here. Please, stop hurting Jordan, she only wanted to help you."

"Mikey, can you look at me?" Alex waited until the delusional man turned back to her. "I know you're scared and upset right now, but I need you to loosen your grip on Jordan, okay? She can't breathe right now. Can you do that for me?" Michael obeyed just enough to ease the pressure on Jordan's windpipe. She dragged in a ragged breath. "That's good...that's good. Thank you, Mikey. Now, can you tell me what happened? Why were you fighting with the others?"

"They tried to take the scissors from me. I went into the office to ask Jordy for a cough drop, but she wasn't in there. I saw the scissors on the desk, and remembered that I had a picture I wanted to cut out."

"Okay, I understand. You're not going to be in trouble for fighting, Mikey. Can you let Jordan go? Please?"

Michael stared at Alex for a minute, looking desperate and confused. His breathing was ragged, and his eyes darted around the room, locking on to each person in the room. The security guard standing closest to them took a step forward, drawing Michael's attention once more, and the man snarled. "Get away from me! You stay back, you want to shoot me! All of you want to hurt me! I won't let you hurt me!"

Jordan gave a strangled gasp, and Alex cried: "Stop! Get out of here, now! You're making it worse! Get the hell out of here, get an ambulance here, now!" Her eyes locked with her best friend's, and tears filled her eyes. "Mikey, please, I'm begging you, stop. You're hurting her, and she just wants to help you, okay? Just let her go."

"I can't stop! If I let her go, they're going to shoot me! I hurt her because they want to hurt me!"

The blades of the scissors dug deeper into Jordan's side, and the brunette whimpered. Blood started to soak her shirt. Her hand dropped to Michael's wrist, keeping a loose grip. "M-Mikey, please...stop. I don't want anything to happen to you. P-please, just let me go. It's okay, you'll be safe, they won't hurt you." The man shook his head desperately, and abruptly embedded the scissors deep in her side. Jordan sobbed in agony, clinging to both of his arms and struggling to keep her feet under her.

"You are all trying to trick me. I know what you're doing...I know you work for the rogue police. Stop lying to me," he growled in her ear. Her knees gave out, and his grip around her throat tightened in an effort to keep her upright. Jordan scrambled to pull her head up far enough to clear her airway, but her legs would no longer hold her.

"Michael," Alex snapped, voice suddenly full of authority. "If you don't let her go right now, this officer is going to be forced to shoot you. We are not involved with any rogue police agency. We are here to *help* you, but we cannot allow you to keep hurting her. Put the scissors down and let her go."

The cocking of a gun drew Jordan's fading attention, and she prayed that her patient listened to Alex. "Please...Mikey, listen. Please." Darkness clouded her vision, and all she knew in the next moment was that she was falling. Whether Michael had let her go or had been killed, she had no idea. She could no longer hear anything, and within seconds, she didn't feel *anything* as unconsciousness took over.

Chapter Fourteen

-Chase-

"Chase, hi, this is Alex. Look, I'm sorry for calling you like this, but...I need you to call me back as soon as you can. It's an emergency."

Fear shot through Chase, and his heart leapt into his throat as he listened to the message he'd just missed while coming out of the locker room at work. As he rushed to his car he hit redial, and felt his blood pressure rise with each passing second until Alex finally answered.

"Hey, Chase...look, I know things are tense between you and Jordan right now, but you should get to the hospital as soon as you can."

"Alex, *what happened?*"

Her sigh sounded tired and sad, and it made every muscle in his body tense. Images flashed in his mind of car accidents, horrible illnesses, and another image that threatened to derail him: the man that had already beaten her down emotionally, standing over her after hurting her physically. *"There was an incident with one of our patients. She was stabbed. It's pretty bad."*

"I'll be right there."

Chase couldn't bring himself to care about speed limits or stop signs as he rushed to the hospital. Scenarios continued to run through his head in fast forward, and he couldn't stop thinking *what if this is it? What if she dies and the last thing she knew was that I was avoiding her? Even if she ended up with Adam again...I won't be able to forgive myself if she thinks I didn't love her.*

As soon as he pulled into the emergency room parking lot, he spotted Alex's car and pulled in beside it. Chase hardly registered the sound of his own pounding footsteps on the pavement as he made a beeline for the entrance. He made it inside in record time, and came to a skidding stop directly in front of Alex, who'd clearly been waiting for him at the registration desk. "What happened? What do you know? Is she going to be okay?" The last question came out as more of a wheeze he threw out one after another without pausing for a breath.

Alex put a placating hand on his shoulder, and gestured for him to follow her. Antsy, he had to reign himself in as she led him down random hallways to a smaller waiting room. No one else was in the room. It made Chase feel anxious. "She was stabbed in the side. They haven't told me much, we just got here half an hour ago and they had to take her up to surgery to repair the damage. The doctor will come in as soon as they know anything."

"Alex, how did she look? How bad was it?" Chase's eyes pleaded with her to tell him something, *anything* that would let him know that she was going to make it.

"She was really pale; she'd lost a lot of blood. It took a long time to get him to let her go, but the doctor seemed optimistic that they'd be able to fix it. He said it seemed like the scissors missed anything major."

The guardsman ran his hands through his hair, and felt his arms start to shake. Realizing that he was crashing quickly from his adrenaline high now that he had nowhere else to *go*, he dropped numbly into a chair. Alex sat next to him, and rubbed his back gently. "You should not be the one comforting *me* right now. I'm sorry, she's *your* best friend. Are you okay, Alex?"

Chase looked over to her, waiting for her to meet his gaze. Once she did, just like that, her strong facade shattered before his eyes. Tears spilled onto her cheeks, and a sob shook her body. Chase wrapped his arms around her, and rocked her gently. "He's dead...the client that stabbed her. He's dead. I couldn't do anything to help her, and the idiots that forgot all of their training kept making it worse...and...and he's *dead*. Jordan's going to be devastated," she moaned.

Chase kissed the top of her head, and stroked her hair. His eyes took in the basic decorations on the walls around him. He idly thought that the lack of warmth in the room did nothing to make anxious and scared family members feel consoled.

"It'll be okay. We'll get her through it...we'll get *both* of you through this. She's strong, she'll pull through. There was nothing that you could do; you're not trained to deal with violent clients with weapons," he soothed. Chase found himself mildly impressed with his own ability to shut down his emotions in that moment; Alex and Jordan were the counselors, the ones trained to compartmentalize their own feelings. "How...how did one of your patients even get a pair of scissors?"

Alex sniffed, and shook her head. "Someone left a pair of scissors on the staff desk. The patient went in to talk to Jordan, but she hadn't gotten back from rounds in the cafeteria yet. He saw the scissors, and decided to take them for a craft he'd been working on in group. A couple of the other patients saw them in his hand, tried to take them. She was trying to talk them down from a fight when one of our new guys got a little overeager, and set him off. He was seriously paranoid, so he thought we were all trying to hurt him. Jordan was just the closest one to him at the time."

"I'm sorry that you had to see one of your patients...uh..." he hesitated, unable to finish his sentence. He cleared his throat and Alex gave him a sad smile. "Jordan didn't see?"

"I don't know," Alex admitted. "She didn't react to the gunshot. I...I think she was unconscious when it happened."

Chase clenched his jaw and squeezed his eyes shut to rein in his emotions at the thought. "I-" He cleared his throat when his voice cracked. "I think that might have been for the best." They sat in silence for a moment, comforting one another. "Where is Brian?" Chase questioned softly.

Alex leaned back, wiping her tears away hastily. "He...he was still out on the truck, so he won't get my message until he gets back into the station. Hopefully he'll be getting back soon. I'm expecting him to call any minute."

A thought struck Chase, and he found himself struggling to voice his next question. "What about...what about Adam?" As much as he didn't want to hear the answer, or see him standing over her bed, playing the part of doting husband, Chase knew that the man needed to be notified.

Alex looked up at him with an unreadable expression in her eyes. "I-I don't have his number," she murmured. He gave her a confused look, and raised a questioning eyebrow at her. What was she not telling him? "Don't, Chase. Please. You and Jordan need to have a conversation when she wakes up, okay?"

"Alex," he pleaded. The woman simply shook her head, refusing to budge. Chase sighed. "Fine. But he should know either way. I can call the base and put someone in touch with him."

"I think the hospital has her emergency contact information on file. They can contact him if they want to," Alex insisted. Chase shook his head, a flicker of hope fighting to shine through his fear and grief. *Why would she be so unwilling to reach out to Jordan's husband when they'd just reconciled?*

Alex's phone started buzzing on the table beside her, causing both of them to jump. "It's Brian. I'm going to go find him and bring him up here. Are you going to be okay for a few minutes?" Chase nodded silently, and she squeezed his shoulder before disappearing out of the room. Chase dropped his head into his hands, elbows resting on his knees. "What am I going to do if I lose her? Why the hell was I willing to let her walk away from me?" he muttered to himself, pulling at strands of hair caught between his fingers. "God, protect her. Get her through this, I am begging you. She is strong...she is a fighter. Make sure she remembers that. Don't let her give up. I don't care if she's just meant to be my friend; I *need* her in my life."

He stayed in that same position, he couldn't tell how long. His thoughts bounced around, incoherent to his own mind, but he bared his soul to God, pleading for more time. He knew it was all out of his hands; it was all in the plan of an incredible force far greater than he could ever fathom.

"Hey, man...what's wrong? Did you hear something else?" Brian's voice pulled him back to the present, and Chase wiped his face before looking up to see matching looks of trepidation on the couple's faces.

"No...no, nothing new. I just needed to have a conversation with God. I'm sorry, I didn't mean to scare you guys."

"It's okay, Chase. How are you holding up, man?" Brian fell into the seat next to him and clapped a hand on his shoulder. Chase gave him a weak smile.

"I'll be great as soon as we know that she's okay." Chase sighed and shook his head. "I can't stop thinking about how I ignored and avoided her all week. She tried to reach out to me after she told me about her planned meeting with Adam...but I never let her tell me what happened. I should have been there for her, I should have been the *friend* I am supposed to be. I can't imagine how she must have been feeling...finally moving on from her abusive relationship, only to have it thrown back into her face when he decides he's bored with the other woman. I should have supported her no matter what. Now, if something happens and she doesn't make it through this," he shook his head, "that's all she's going to know. That I abandoned her when she needed me."

"Hey," Alex murmured, placing her hand on his knee. Chase looked up at her, seated on the opposite side of him from her husband, and he saw tears in her eyes. "She knew-*knows* that you care about her. She understands that you needed time. She respects you too much to not understand that. And she *will* make it through this, and then you can take all the time that you need to apologize for what happened this week, okay? Everything is going to be okay."

Chase nodded. "Yes, ma'am," he muttered, cracking a small smile. "Will you guys pray with me?" The two nodded in unison, and all of them joined hands and bowed their heads. "Heavenly Father, we lift Jordan up to you right now. Please protect her, give her strength to fight through this. God, she is a passionate follower of Yours, and has so much more inside of her to devote to You. You call us to be bold in our prayers, so we come to You boldly tonight. Guide the hands of the doctors, and bring her back to us. In Jesus' precious name we pray...amen."

Alex pushed herself to her feet once he was finished. "I'm going to go and find something to eat Do you guys need anything?" Both Chase and Brian shook their heads. "Okay, call me if you hear anything new."

The two men sat in silence for a while after Alex left. Brian turned his attention from the television to his friend. "I understand why you needed your space, Chase, and so did Jordan. You know that, right?"

Chase shook his head in self-deprecation. "No. *I* don't even understand why I needed space. Whether it's as a friend or as a girlfriend, I know that I want her in my life. I care about her too much to let her walk away."

"You're going to have to forgive yourself. She's going to need you one way or another to get through this. Even if things work out with Adam, they've got a long road ahead of them, and it's going to be really hard on her. She's going to need your support to survive."

"She doesn't need me," he murmured. "Adam won't like me being in the picture as it is, but she's strong enough to get through that on her own."

"You underestimate your significance in her life. She won't let him push you away from her. He'll try, because that's just part of who Adam is, but she wouldn't let it happen." Both men looked up when Alex stepped back into the room with a small bag of chips in her hand.

"If Adam is still who he used to be, why would he be able to last another go-round with her? He couldn't take care of her before, let alone now that she found herself and has learned how to stand up for herself."

Brian didn't respond, looking at his friend sympathetically. It was the same look that Alex had given him earlier, and it made him feel uncomfortable. He *hated* being out of the loop, especially about someone so important.

"Family of Jordan Davis?" The three jumped at the nurse's voice, and Alex stepped forward. "Alexandra Coale?" She nodded eagerly. "Jordan is out of surgery. She is going to be sore, and will need to take a couple of weeks to allow herself to recover, especially because she needed a transfusion from the blood loss, but she is resting comfortably and should be just fine. I will come back in a few minutes when she starts waking up, and you can go back to see her."

The exhausted sighs of relief filled the room, and Alex turned to Brian, who'd stepped up behind her. He wrapped her in a tight hug, and Alex sobbed. "Thank you," she whispered. Brian rubbed her back.

Chase squeezed his eyes shut and allowed his head to *thunk* back against the wall. *Thank you, Lord.* A firm touch on his knee jolted him from his impending spiral. Alex was crouched before him with a kind look on her face.

"You should go in to be with her first. Like I said, you guys have some things to talk about. Just get it out of the way," she insisted with a tender smile. Chase nodded, and took her hands. The friends stood together, and she hugged him as tightly as Brian had hugged her. "She's okay...she's okay. You'll make it right." He nodded wordlessly, and then pulled back. All three of them fought to reign in their emotions, laughing wetly at one another as they hastily brushed away tears. "She will never let us live it down if she knows we were all blubbering messes over a little cut."

"*Little cut,*" Brian scoffed, his voice lacking any venom.

"She's waking up, you can come back now," the nurse stated from the doorway. Chase glanced at his friends one last time to make sure they were okay with him going in alone, and both nodded without hesitation.

As the nurse led him down the hallway to her room, Chase couldn't fight an overwhelming sense of anxiety. *What if she hated him for not talking to her? What if they'd just been trying to make him feel better in case she never woke up?* He heard her voice before he saw her, and everything else suddenly fell away. A tremulous smile pulled at his lips, and the nurse smiled at him and gestured for the room just ahead of them.

"Miss Davis, are you ready for a visitor?" Her smile faltered, however, as they stepped into the doorway.

Jordan wasn't alone. Chase's heart squeezed in his chest, and he instinctively stepped back as she looked up. The nurse glanced over at him in confusion. Sympathy quickly took over as she realized that Chase recognized the man standing at Jordan's bedside, and didn't want Jordan to see him in light of the new visitor's presence. Chase dropped his eyes to the floor, and immediately started to back away. He heard the nurse say something else to Jordan as he turned to bolt, but didn't stay to figure out what it was. He barely even hesitated long enough for Brian and Alex to see him pass the waiting room.

"Chase!" Brian called, jogging after him. "Chase, where are you going? What happened?" Concern was clear in his friend's voice, and that just made everything feel ten times worse.

"I-I shouldn't have come. Tell her I'm glad that she's okay. I...I thought I would be okay with it, but I just can't yet. I need some more time."

"More time? More time for what? Chase, come back!" He ignored his friend, turning the corner and willing him not to follow. He needed to clear his head.

Chapter Fifteen

Awareness slowly returned to Jordan, first in the form of the obnoxious beeping that wouldn't *stop*. She hated that kind of sound as it was, let alone when she was coming out of a darkness that refused to let her go. Once she adjusted to the blaring noise, she noticed the glaring light piercing through her eyelids. Once *that* registered, everything else seemed to come into focus a little faster. She tightened her hands in an effort to regain her control and bearings. A scratchy linen met her fingertips. Jordan forced her eyes to open. Nothing made sense.

As soon as her eyelids cracked open, they slammed shut against the light. Ouch...too bright. Way too bright. "Ow," she moaned quietly.

"Easy there, killer. Take your time." The sun suddenly cut out, leaving her in blissful shade. Jordan tested her vision again, and was grateful to be able to open her eyes enough to take in her surroundings. A hospital room. *Huh.*

"What happened?" she croaked, turning to the shadow near the doorway.

"There was an incident at work. They didn't give me the full details, but they had to rush you here and called me when they found out you had my insurance."

Suddenly, realization barreled into her. Memories of what happened at work...*what happened with Adam.* Adam. The man standing in her doorway, talking to her like nothing had changed between them. The 'sun' had been the hospital room lights, which apparently Adam had turned off for her. "Adam..."

"I'm not going anywhere, I'll be here to help get you back on your feet. You've got to take it easy, okay? We'll get through this together."

"Adam."

"I've already got leave lined up to get you through the first week. The doctor said you'd need to be off your feet for a few days until your side starts to heal. I told them you'd want to leave as soon as you're awake, so they agreed to let me take you home as long as I keep an eye on you."

"*Adam!*" Jordan hissed, triggering a coughing fit from her overly dry throat. Muscles in her abdomen clenched as she hacked, and she doubled over in pain. She could tell that the sensation was seriously dulled by pain medication, but it was still enough to steal her breath away. Adam rubbed her back comfortingly, and she feebly tried to push his hand away. "Don't. You don't get to make decisions for me...you don't get to speak for me here. You don't get to come in and pretend like you're this caring, doting husband after everything you've put me through."

"Jordan, you need to calm down. Everything is going to be fine, just let me take care of you." He raised his hands to placate her, but all it did was make her skin crawl. He was acting as though she were overreacting, and the fact that he was doing it while she was incapacitated made her sick to her stomach. He was *relentless*, and absolutely shameless in his attempt to assert his dominance.

"You need to *leave*, Adam. Now."

"Jordan, please. Relax. You're being ridiculous."

"Miss Davis, are you ready for a visitor?" her nurse asked brightly from the doorway. Jordan looked over and watched the smile fall from her face as she looked at Adam and then turned her attention to something in the hall. When she looked back into the room, the nurse became visibly concerned at the sight of Jordan leaning forward and clutching her stomach. "I'm glad to see that you're awake, but you shouldn't be sitting up just yet."

"I-can you please see him out? I don't want him here. At all. I have someone else I'd rather be here. Could I borrow a phone?" Adam glared furiously at her, but Jordan met his stare without flinching. Maybe it was the drugs, leaving her feeling slightly disconnected from the world, but she was entirely unaffected by his agitation.

"I was not aware any other visitors had been allowed back, do you know him?" The woman stepped into the room, suspicious eyes fixed on Adam.

"I'm her *husband*," Adam snapped. The nurse raised an eyebrow at him, though Jordan couldn't tell if it was what he said or his attitude. Her side twinged sharply in protest of her position pulling at stitches.

Jordan sighed, gently easing herself back as the nurse stepped further into the room and pressed a few buttons on her IV. Warmth spread through her arm, and the sting dissipated from her wound. The nurse watched her face carefully, and

Jordan was grateful for her attention. "We are *separated*. Getting divorced. He does not speak for me, and I would prefer not to see him. I certainly do not want to be leaving here before my doctor says that I am good to go, and I *will not* be leaving with *him*."

Without hesitation, the nurse turned to face Adam, who looked to be barely containing his rage. "It's time you left, sir. The patient needs rest, and I cannot have that impeded by visitors that are not wanted at this time." He growled and stomped out of the room. Only then did Jordan feel herself relax. "I am sorry, Jordan. The other staff must have spoken to him while I was in the waiting room with the young lady that came in with you; they must've assumed that he was your next of kin."

Jordan shook her head. "I don't blame them at all. He's still listed as my emergency contact, I guess. They did what they were supposed to do."

The nurse smiled at her warmly as she checked over all of the machines and IV bags around her. "My name is Jennifer. Would you like to see the couple waiting for you?"

Jordan felt her spirits lift at the mention of her best friends. "Yes, please, send them in. They are okay," she teased lightly. Jennifer grinned and ducked out of the room. Less than two minutes later, familiar, warm faces entered her doorway. "Alex, Brian, I am so, *so* glad you're here."

"We wouldn't be anywhere else, Jordy. We're just glad you're okay. I was so terrified after everything." Alex took her hand and squeezed tightly.

The reference to the incident that put her in the hospital brought a wave of memories. "Oh, my God...Michael? Is...is he?" She stared up at Alex's face, and felt her heart twist when she didn't answer right away. Tears burned her eyes. "No," she whimpered. Emotions seemed to escape her after that, and she suddenly felt numb. "They just...they handled everything all wrong. They made the situation worse. If they'd just let us handle it, we could have talked him down. We could've kept all of this from happening. We could have...we could have..." A sob wrenched from her chest, and Alex wrapped her in a firm hug.

"You did the best that you could. We both did. There's nothing else that we could have done to stop what happened. You can't think about that anymore; you need to focus on recovering, okay? We're going to stay with you until you're ready to go home, and then you'll stay with us until you're back to 100%."

"Sammy! Oh, poor Sammy is probably freaking out by now..."

"Don't worry," Brian assured. "I already picked her up and took her over to our place. She's hanging out with my mother and the kids."

Jordan sagged in relief. "Thank you so much. I don't know what I did to deserve you guys." Alex finally let her go, and leaned back. "Adam was here. They...they called him as the next of kin, and he tried to have me signed out as soon as I woke up so that he could 'take care of me'. Jennifer was quick to get him out of here as soon as I let her know that it was not kosher between us."

"He's lucky we didn't see him, or he would've been in a bed of his own," Brian growled. Something seemed to strike him. "That must have been why Chase took off."

"Chase was here?" Jordan gasped with surprise, trying to sit up. Alex pushed her back down, giving her a stern look when she cringed in pain.

"I called him as soon as they took you back. He made it here in record time. When Jennifer told us that you were waking up, we sent him up to see you first, to give you guys some time to talk. He made a quick exit not long after that, and wouldn't say why he was leaving."

"I need to see him," Jordan insisted. "Can you call him?"

Alex shook her head, "I've tried, several times. His phone is going straight to voicemail."

Jordan shook her head sadly, cursing her soon-to-be ex husband for once again getting in between what would actually be a *healthy* relationship for her. "I know where he would've gone. I need to go to him...I can't let him think that Adam is back in my life. Not anymore. Please, will you help me?"

"Absolutely not! Are you insane? Jordan, you just woke up!"

"And they said that I will be fine! I'm nicely stitched up, I've got some pain meds in me. At least if you drive me you know that I'm going to get there and back safely. I'll come right back, I just need him to know that I've chosen him. I'm going with or without you," she promised. Alex stared her down, but eventually growled out her frustration and turned to find the nurse.

Both women returned quickly. "Jordan, I cannot advise you leaving right now. Coming back or not, you are still under the effects of the sedation and heavy duty painkillers. You could seriously hurt yourself and undo the work from the surgery," Jennifer insisted.

"Look, I understand that it's a really bad idea, I do. I will sign whatever papers you need me to. If something goes wrong I won't hold you accountable at all, and I will be gone an hour tops. I promise. I'll be right back. But I *have* to see him, and I *have* to tell him the truth about my ex."

Jennifer stared at her forlornly for a long moment, before turning to Alex. "I can only agree to this if you are with her at all times. If she so much as tweaks her stitches, I don't care if she gets called to a tea party with Tom Holland, she is coming *directly* back here, do you understand?" Alex nodded, resigned to the fact that Jordan had made her decision. Jennifer turned back to Jordan. "If you're talking about the young man that I think you are, I saw the look on his face when he saw your ex. Don't let him go, okay?"

Jordan teared up at the thought of Chase seeing what must've looked like a sweet reunion. "I just hope he gives me a chance to explain everything to him," she murmured. Jennifer nodded, placed a supportive hand on her leg, and left the room to get the paperwork she needed.

"I hope you know how much we all love you, crazy girl," Brian commented. Jordan looked up to him, and smiled tenderly at the 'protective dad,' crossed-arms look he was giving her. "Otherwise you would be totally on your own with this crazy adventure of yours. I am pretty sure this is 100% against the rules for this hospital to let you leave and come back like that."

"That's fine, I'll deal with whatever I have to deal with. He's worth it."

Chapter Sixteen

-Chase-

Chase tore pieces of seaweed apart, allowing his frustration to channel into the innocent sea vegetation. He wasn't sure how much more of this roller coaster he could stand; meeting Jordan and Adam, watching him treat her like an afterthought, watching him try to break her, only to be left in awe of how she'd persevered. Drawing close to her before losing her to her abusive husband. Finding out that she could die, having a glimmer of hope that he hadn't lost her to Adam after all…just to walk in on Adam holding her hand as she woke up from surgery.

Everything screamed at him to be patient, that there was something missing and that God wouldn't have brought him this far just to rip it all away just like that...but his heart was hurting. It was bad enough to lose her when he hadn't even been able to be with her, but to lose her to the man that had spent so long trying to break her? It just wasn't fair. For either of them. He wasn't sure he could watch them together, seeing how he'd treated her the few times he'd ever seen them in the same place. As easy as it was for Adam to be cruel to her, it was incredibly difficult for Chase to believe that he'd changed enough in the short time since that day to deserve a second chance.

Chase knew he wasn't perfect - far from it - but he knew that he had a responsibility as a man to protect the woman in his life. Beside the Biblical order for a husband to love his wife as *Christ loved the Church,* simple respect as a man for his significant other demands love and care. The thought of causing her pain made Chase nauseous, and the thought of Jordan giving Adam the chance to cause her pain again made him *angry*. He didn't think he would be able to sit by silently and watch the woman she had become melt away again under her husband's cruel words.

"If you keep thinking that hard, smoke's going to come out of your ears."

Chase twisted around to see a too-pale Jordan leaning on Alex as they carefully made their way down the beach. He gave the latter an incredulous look, which was met with an exasperated glare. "Don't look at me, she was coming whether I helped her or not. I'm going to give you guys some privacy. Bring her straight back to the hospital when you're done talking?"

Chase nodded wordlessly at her, jumping to his feet to take over the task of supporting Jordan. He watched Alex leave before taking a deep breath and turning his attention to the woman at his side. "Come on, Jaybird, let's get you off your feet," he murmured. Jordan leaned heavily on him as she settled into the sand, and as soon as she let him go her hand moved to her injured side. "Are you okay?"

The brunette nodded, but took several slow breaths through her nose. Chase watched her face closely until she finally opened her eyes and looked at him. "You know, this would have been much easier if you'd just *answer your phone,*" she teased. Chase knew there was no real upset in her words. It didn't stop him from feeling guilty.

Even if she got back together with Adam, he had no reason or right to treat her any differently than he'd done in the past. "I left my phone in the car. I needed some time to think."

"After seeing Adam holding my hand, right?" Chase's surprised look was answer enough. "I sent him away as soon as I was aware that he was there. The hospital called him because he was listed as my next of kin on my ID card, but I told them I didn't want him anywhere near me."

The words had Chase's heart speeding up. "What about trying to fix things?" he whispered.

Jordan gave him a wry smile. "Had you answered your phone in the last week and a half, and had you not avoided me at church, I would have been able to tell you. Adam is still exactly who he's always been. He stood me up, and then told me that I was bitter and angry. He just wanted a way to turn it into my fault, and when I stood my ground about needing a few days to cool down before trying to meet again, he got exactly that. He didn't like the thought of me having any control, let alone me standing up for myself. It's really over, Chase. For good."

Chase couldn't believe what he was hearing. "W-what about Cassandra?"

Jordan smiled sadly. "After what happened that day at the beach, she saw him for who he is. She ended it with him and is transferring to Sitka." This new information gave Chase a minimal sense of respect for the woman; while she did the right thing in the end, she'd still been beyond wrong for continuing with a relationship with a man who was for one, still legally married and for two, the husband of someone she'd once considered a close friend.

Chase was silent for a long moment. He stared blankly at his hands, resting on his knees, and wondered why he'd been put into the middle of this whole mess. A gentle hand covered his own. He turned his eyes up to meet Jordan's green gaze. "I'm sorry that I shut you out. It wasn't fair," he murmured.

Tears shone in her eyes when she shook her head. "No, Chase...what happened wasn't fair to *you*. You have been nothing but wonderful to me, and you didn't deserve having the rug ripped out from under you like that. I don't blame you for needing to separate yourself from the situation."

"When Alex called me to let me know what happened to you," he shuddered at the memory, "all I could think about was the fact that the last thing you'd have known from me would be that I walked away from you and avoided you when you would have potentially needed your friends most." Jordan scooted closer to him, and tucked herself against his side. Chase wrapped an arm around her shoulders, soaking in her solid presence with him and sending thanks to God for protecting her, both physically and emotionally. He pressed a tender kiss to the top of her head, and rested his cheek on her hair. "I'm sorry you had to go through more stress with Adam, but I can't bring myself to be sorry that it really is over."

Jordan chuckled, pressing her face into his shoulder as her amusement turned into a fit of giggles. "Oooh," she whimpered, "don't make me laugh, ow..." After a moment she reined in her emotions and took a breath. "You and me both. Does that make us horrible people?"

"Me, probably." He nodded, sending her a wry grin. "You? No way. You suffered more than I know, so I can only imagine how much of a relief it was to have a *definitive* answer to whether or not he'd actually changed. That's God's work, telling you without a doubt that you are doing the right thing."

"Can we just stay here a while?" Jordan murmured, tracing random shapes with her fingers on his chest. Chase smiled sadly.

"You shouldn't be here as it is, Jay. Alex is counting on me to get you back to the hospital in one piece. You are looking more and more like a ghost every minute. We need to get you back soon. How much pain are you in right now?"

Jordan was silent for a moment, the lazy circles now being drawn on his shoulder the only indication that she hadn't dozed off. "I, uh...I guess I'm pretty sore," she replied.

"Oh, *pretty sore*, huh?" he teased lightly. "Come on, let's get you back so you can get some of the good drugs." Chase waited for her to pull herself into an upright position, and then jumped to his feet. He offered her his hands, and eased her carefully to standing. Jordan wavered for a moment, so Chase wrapped an arm around her back and held both of her hands.

She allowed her weight to settle against him. He held her steady while she breathed slowly. "You okay? Cause, if not...I could always carry you." Jordan huffed in amusement, but couldn't seem to find her voice. She shook her head firmly. "Hey, I'm serious. If you overdid it, if you can't walk, I can get you to the car." His voice was suddenly void of humor, but she shook her head again. "Okay, okay...but you miss one step, and I'm taking over. Understood?"

The pair made their way slowly and carefully back to his car. Chase kept a firm grip on her waist with one hand, and reacted instantly when she started to stumble. His grip tightened, and his right hand released hers, prepared to brace her if she was unable to right herself. "I'm fine," she growled before he could even speak. Chase could tell that she was becoming frustrated with her limitations from her injury. Jordan leaned away from him as if to step out of his reach.

"Jordan, you have been out of surgery less than four hours. You had to have a blood transfusion, and you have stitches in your side. Cut yourself a break. If you overdo this and pull your stitches, you're going to end up in the hospital a lot longer than you thought. I am here to help you, I'm not judging you or thinking that you are weak because you can't sprint up the sand. *Let me help you.*"

The abrupt stern tone of his voice seemed to catch Jordan by surprise. She finally relented. She leaned herself against him once again, and reached for his hand with her right one. She laced their fingers together, and nodded to let him know that she was ready to move again. Anytime she hesitated, he allowed her to take a moment to breathe through the pain, and remained stoic throughout. It took all of his willpower not to take over, but he knew she needed the autonomy to move of her own volition.

By the time they made it to his Jeep, Jordan was visibly exhausted. He helped her ease into the passenger seat, and jogged around to jump in behind the wheel. When he glanced over, warmth and affection flooded him. That fast, she'd rested her head against the window and fallen asleep.

Chapter Seventeen

The next time Jordan stirred, she felt warm and heavy. A low hum rumbled in her chest as she fought to push away the fog of sleep.

"You're fine, take your time. Don't give yourself a headache trying to force it," a gentle voice whispered. The amusement present in the tone helped to dispel any concerns, so Jordan allowed herself to relax and wake up gradually. "That's my girl."

Her conversation with Chase at the beach, Adam showing up at her bedside...it all resurfaced, and helped bring clarity back to her. "Why do I feel worse now than I did the last time I woke up here?" she muttered. Chase's warm chuckle had her prying her eyes open. The sight of him lounging in the chair beside her bed stoked warmth in her chest.

He leaned forward and held a straw to her lips. She immediately drank, savoring the cool relief of the water coating her throat. "That would be because you hadn't seriously overdone it last time you woke up in here," he admonished lightly. Jordan met his gaze, and could read the exasperation in his dark eyes. "You tore your stitches, and had started to bleed through the bandages by the time we got back here. Jennifer is less than thrilled about letting you go out, by the way. Coming back in with you too out of it to walk on your own had her in a fit."

"Too out of it to walk on my own?" Jordan questioned softly. "I don't remember waking up at all."

Chase straightened out his legs and planted them flat on the floor. "Yeah, you woke up a few times. You weren't too keen on me lifting you out of the car to put you in the wheelchair. I think you'd just put too much into coming to the lighthouse and you couldn't fight the drugs that were still in your system. So you're in here for another day or two, until they feel confident that your stitches aren't going to tear again. Then you're going to be staying with Alex and Brian until you're healed enough to get around on your own."

Jordan nodded, holding his gaze for a long moment before she finally had to drag her eyes away. "I'm sorry that I put you through that. I-I know that what I did was dumb, and I should have just waited for you to call me back...but I couldn't stand the thought of you believing that I was back with Adam. I was...I was *so angry* at him for what he did. I was *so frustrated* that he was here when I woke up; that you'd had to see that, and that by the time I was able to tell them otherwise, you'd already gone. I know it's going to take me a long time to get over everything he did, but knowing that you understand the truth now, I'm okay with that. And I'm okay with this, with being here a little bit longer."

Chase raised an eyebrow at her, but couldn't keep the affection from his face. "I could have done without you setting yourself back, but I'm glad to know the truth as well. I couldn't wrap my head around the idea that you would be subjecting yourself to him again, especially knowing that he hadn't changed at all considering how he'd acted, what, three days before? He was an absolute jerk, and there was no way that he changed that fast. Seeing him in here with you made my skin crawl, but I was determined to keep my mouth shut if that's what you felt you needed to do."

"Yeah, well, thankfully, he will be a distant memory soon. I'm sure it'll be a fight getting those papers, but I'll be keeping on his case until he gets them submitted. I'm done playing the pushover, I'm done letting him drag his feet. It's time for me to move on with my life."

Chase smiled at her, and took her hand. Jordan looked down at their laced fingers, and felt butterflies in her stomach. "I don't want to make this more difficult for you, but after all of this, you're going to have a hard time getting rid of me. I'm apologizing in advance, I'll try to behave."

The small smile that she gave him was tired. "I don't want you to go anywhere, but we are going to have to work hard to keep from crossing that line until the papers come in. I don't want to give him anything to use against you. He can try to accuse me of whatever he wants. I'm not in the military. I can't be held to the UCMJ. But I'm not going to give him a chance of dragging you down with him. He'll probably try, and if he does, I will tell the truth about what he's done, and he'll have much worse than divorce lawyers to deal with." She stared into his brown eyes. "But nothing can come back against you."

"Hey," Chase murmured, standing over her and cradling her face with both hands. "You don't need to be worrying about me. We're keeping it platonic for now, but if he wants to come after me, I welcome it. He could use a reminder of what it means to be a man."

Jordan rolled her eyes good-naturedly, and pulled his hands from her cheeks. "If he's going to get that reminder, it will *not* be coming from you, mister. You need to stay as far away from him as you can until your job won't be on the line. He will answer for what he's done. Just...just not like that. Not to you."

"Okay, okay. Look, I'll be here until Alex gets here after work. We're not going to leave you alone while Adam knows where you are. Get some rest, we'll figure everything else out soon enough, okay?" He raised her hand and pressed a tender kiss to her knuckles.

"Alright, fine," Jordan grumbled. She grinned up at him before settling into her pillow and surrendering herself to the draw of blissful unawareness.

***

-Chase-

"How has she been doing?" Alex whispered, rousing Chase from a light doze. The fireman looked up at her, and smiled at the affection on her face as she looked at Jordan. The injured woman was still fast asleep, had been for several uninterrupted hours.

"So far so good. She's been out for a while; after everything, she certainly needed the sleep."

"And there's no sign of unfriendly faces?"

"All clear. How are things on the work front?"

Alex sighed, and his heart went out to her. It had taken her some time to feel comfortable returning to work after the incident, and he hadn't gotten to talk to her in length since then. "It's...it's hard. I don't think she's going to be able to go back after she gets better. I don't know how I'm going to keep it up myself; being there with the same people that killed Michael and landed Jordan in the hospital, knowing nothing is really changing...it's just too much. I can't do it. I'm starting to look for a new job."

"And the guy that left the scissors out for him to find?" His jaw tensed, and Alex shook her head.

"They aren't doing anything about David. The fact that Michael got the scissors in the first place has kind of been overlooked in light of the fact that he was killed and a staff member was put in the hospital. They have been having meetings left and right talking about self defense and how to safely de-escalate a situation with a client, but they haven't talked once about preventing the clients from *getting* a weapon in the first place. I just...I feel like there's something missing there. Something that they're hiding, some reason that they haven't talked about what led to the situation."

Chase tilted his head to the side as he considered what Alex said. He was relieved to hear that she was going to start looking for other work; the thought of his friend continuing to work in a place that had nearly gotten her best friend killed was almost as nauseating as the idea of Jordan going back there herself. Especially if the carelessness that led to the situation wasn't dealt with. "If they're going to just let it go, you don't need to be waiting around for someone to screw up again. The sooner you are both done with that place, the better."

Alex nodded. "I hear you. Why don't you get out of here, go get some rest. I'm off work tomorrow, so I can be here during the day too. I'll be here until you get off work."

Chase pushed himself to his feet, and found himself unable to tear his eyes away from Jordan's serene face. After seeing her under such stress for so long, to see her at peace stirred up feelings of intense affection and protectiveness. His fingers tucked strands of hair behind her ear almost reverently. Jordan stirred when his lips brushed against her forehead, and she blinked blearily up at him. "Alex is here," he whispered. "I'll be back tomorrow afternoon, okay? Maybe by then we'll know when you can go home. Don't push it while I'm gone, understood?" She nodded and managed an affectionate eye roll.

"Okay, Romeo, get out of here," Alex teased. Chase caressed Jordan's face tenderly before turning and pulling Alex into a tight hug. "See you tomorrow, Chase," Alex mumbled as he nearly squished her. He sent a glance over his shoulder to Jordan, winked at her, and ducked out, leaving the women alone.

***

"Hey, Lex, how was work?" Jordan asked, pushing herself up carefully. Her best friend stepped further into the room, and pressed the button on the bed rail to lift the head of the bed. "Ah, thank you."

"Work is a disaster. I'm looking for a new job. They are handling everything completely wrong, and no one is listening to anything that I have to say. As usual."

Jordan shook her head sadly. "You'd think after something like what happened, they would do whatever it took to make sure it never happened again. They...they lost a *patient* for God's sake, how could they be careless about that?" Tears filled her eyes at the thought of Michael. "I can't go back there, Lex. I can't be in those rooms knowing that he's *dead*. He was so scared. He was so confused. He didn't want to hurt me...he *wouldn't* have hurt me if it wasn't for David and Christopher. They were trying to play the hero, but they just made everything *worse*. How can I look at either of them again knowing what they did?"

"Hey," Alex breathed, taking her best friend's hands in her own and settling into the chair beside the bed. "You don't have to go back there. I know Brian, Chase and I want you to stay far away from that place, and will feel much better knowing that you will. Jordy, you have a major case against the psych hospital. Once you are out of here, Brian is going to help you get set up with a lawyer to deal with everything."

Jordan shook her head. "I don't want to sue the hospital, I just want this to be over."

"You know as well as I do, that nothing is going to change unless you go after them where it's going to hurt them. Jordan, we had been warning them for weeks that all of those men were on the verge of acting out. We'd been fighting for self defense training for months, and for better training for new staff to make sure that *things like that never happened.* This was one hundred percent preventable, but they aren't going to change a thing until they are *challenged* and *forced* to do so."

Jordan sighed, and nodded. Alex reached up and wiped the tears from her cheeks. "I hope Brian knows a good lawyer that's ready to go up against a *hospital.*"

"With a case as clear cut as yours? No problem." The women settled back, and eventually fell into easier conversation, passing the time chatting about random topics.

Chapter Eighteen - August

The lines of cans felt strangely daunting as Jordan stared down the aisle before her. Even three weeks after *the incident,* adjusting back to normal was proving to be much more difficult than she'd anticipated. The simplest things seemed to trigger stress and anxiety in her, and she was beyond over it.

"Earth to Jordan..."

Alex's voice cut through her thoughts and drew her attention. "Hey, sorry..."

Understanding filled her best friend's eyes, but she didn't speak the thoughts Jordan could clearly read in her eyes. "We've still got a few things to grab before we head out. What do you say we add some wine to that list and make it a chick flick night?" Jordan nodded with a tight smile, and plucked the list from Alex's grasp.

"Jordan?" Recognition tightened her chest, and Jordan turned to face a woman she'd once called friend...before Adam left.

"Danielle."

"Hey, I...I'm really sorry, but I saw your car in the parking lot and figured I'd try to catch you in here. Adam asked me to get these to you. H-he said that you can mail them in once you're finished." She held out a large envelope to Jordan. As soon as it left her hand, she gave both women a timid smile, and hurried away.

"Well that was...interesting. What's in the envelope?" Alex asked. As she stared at the packet in her hands, realization dawned on Jordan. Based on the sharp intake of breath, Alex wasn't far behind. "The papers." Jordan nodded numbly. "Okay, let's finish up here and head back to your place. We can look them over together, you can get these bad boys signed and on their merry way to the lawyers."

It took them precisely thirty minutes to get home, review the papers, and for Jordan to fill them out. Sliding the envelope into the outgoing mail left her with mixed emotions, but she forced herself to focus on the positives: Adam had finally finished what he'd started, and the light was within view. Soon, the waiting would be over. Soon, she would be free from Adam and able to truly move on with her life.

Jordan wasn't quite sure how she felt as she walked away from the mailbox.

As soon as she made it back inside, Alex handed her a glass of wine and a piece of chocolate. "Okay, so *He's Just Not That Into You?*" Jordan nodded eagerly, and bit into the bittersweet candy with a hum of contentment. "Perfect. You go settle in, I'll get the movie started."

Jordan obeyed the order, and dropped tiredly onto the couch. Her thoughts wandered back to the papers she'd just dropped in the mail, and how conflicted it made her feel. *Is it wrong to feel relieved? Am I as bad as Adam for the happiness that I feel at the thought of moving on with my life? Lord, I need some of your peace right now; I need to remember that I am entirely in Your hands. Forgive me for being angry at Adam, and forgive me for this relief over the end of my marriage.*

The touch of Alex's hand on hers yanked Jordan back into reality, and she looked up into her best friend's concerned eyes. "Sorry," she murmured.

"Jordan, have you thought about talking to someone about everything you've gone through? Both the divorce and the attack by themselves are enough to warrant needing to see a therapist, but to deal with both at the same time is more than someone should have to handle alone."

Tears burned at the back of her eyes, and Jordan dropped her head into her hands. Sobs wracked through her, and she felt Alex wrap her arms around her back. Jordan leaned into her friend's embrace, drawing strength and comfort as she released the pent up emotions she'd been suppressing for too long. "I'm sorry...I'm sorry, Alex. I don't know what to do anymore. I can't let go of the guilt, I can't help but feel like Michael is dead because of me. I can't help but feel relieved about the divorce being finalized. But that makes me just like Adam...that makes me just as wrong as he is!"

"Don't you dare blame yourself for what happened with Adam. Do you hear me? Jordan, *look* at me," Alex insisted firmly. The grieving woman obeyed, tears streaming down her face. "You gave Adam the benefit of the doubt *three days* after he was an absolute jerk to you. You did what you had to do to try to make things right, even though you had a man who was more than willing to take his place. You were willing to sacrifice a man

- that you and I both know God brought into your life - because you were committed to following through with the vow that you made to Adam, but more importantly, to God. You cannot change a man that refuses to see how much he needs God. You could only provide him the chance to prove himself worthy, and you *did.* God did not call you to subject yourself to an abusive man. He called you to be obedient to *Him*, and you were."

She stared into Jordan's eyes until she nodded reluctantly. "And Michael was not your fault either. You didn't leave the scissors out, you didn't set him off. You tried to protect him, you tried to talk him down. We did everything we could to fix it...and you are going to be a big part of making changes in that hospital to make sure it doesn't ever happen again."

Jordan dropped her gaze to the floor, and felt fresh tears fall. "Yeah, I'm suing the psych hospital. I'm going to *benefit* from the death of one of my patients. That's really big of me."

"Jordan, you suing the hospital is the only thing that is going to force them to change their policies. Something *has* to change in how they train their staff, in how they train their *security team* to make sure something like that never happens again. And yes, you are going to get financial compensation for what you went through, but that's not the same as you *benefitting from Michael's death.* They owe you more than they will be able to give you for not listening, for not protecting you from all of this. They can never take back that trauma. They can never take back that scar left behind."

Jordan didn't reply, soaking in her best friend's words and finally letting go of her guilt. She threw her arms around Alex's neck, and felt a huge weight lift off of her shoulders. Even in her most relaxed moments in the last few months, she realized that she'd still carried the heaviness of her guilt over the divorce - and then later the attack - in her heart, and allowed it to hold her back.

"That's my girl, let it out, I'm here. I've got you. You don't have to keep being so strong, that's what your friends are here for. I will always be here to tell you that you're not responsible for what happened to you. I know how much you've been hurting, and I don't want you to keep thinking that you have to hurt alone, okay? Let me help you sometimes. Let *us* help you. Chase wants to be there for you too, whether you are together yet or not." She gently rubbed Jordan's back, not letting go until she felt Jordan start to pull away.

"I know. I'm sorry I haven't been opening up to you about

how I've been feeling. I just...didn't know how to voice it without feeling even worse for sharing something that felt so *wrong*."

Alex smacked her lightly on the arm before pushing herself up and collapsing onto the couch next to her best friend. "You know I'm not going to judge you for anything like that, Jor. You know I'm always going to be honest with you, but I would never add to your pain. I love you. You're my best friend, my *sister*."

Jordan leaned against Alex and dropped her temple to her friend's shoulder. "I know I know...I love you too. Thank you for getting me out of my own head, Lex."

"You're welcome. Now shut it and drink your wine, it's movie time." The pair laughed as the film began to play, and Jordan sent a prayer of gratitude for the lightness that had taken over the space left by the guilt she'd clung to for far too long.

***

"It's probably going to be a little while until we are able to get everything finalized, but they are going to continue to pay your salary in the meantime, and you will be awarded at least two hundred and fifty thousand dollars when all's said and done."

Jordan felt like she'd had the wind knocked out of her, and had to take a moment before she could reply to her lawyer. "W-wow...thank you, Jeff...I really appreciate the update. Do-do I need to appear in court anytime soon?"

"No, if you do, it will be after things are further along, but I'm going to try to settle this first. They don't want to go to trial with me, so I'm expecting them to cooperate. They will have a chance to make it right first, and if I know the director, she will. Otherwise, I will absolutely go to bat for you, and make sure you have to spend as little time in front of a jury as possible. I will let you know if I think it's going to come to that, don't worry."

Jordan nodded, only belatedly realizing that she was on the phone and therefore could not be seen. "Okay. Thank you again, Jeff, you have been amazing. I'll talk to you soon."

After the call ended, Jordan stared numbly at the phone in her hand. Two hundred and fifty thousand dollars. That was more than enough to support her through the last two years of her graduate schooling, which would give her the opportunity she'd been looking for to complete her required internship without having to continue working full time. It was more than

enough to also pay off her existing school loans. *Thank you,
Father...thank you for giving me such an incredible gift from such a
difficult experience.*

Chapter Nineteen - September

Jordan smiled down at Sammy as she pulled the mail from her box. She sifted through a handful of junk mail, and felt her heart stop at the sight of a large manila envelope at the bottom of the stack. She whistled for her companion to follow her, and didn't have to look to know that the dog was following as she made her way back inside. The junk mail was discarded blindly on the table. Her hands shook as she turned the envelope over and pulled it open.

It was official. She was legally divorced. Conflicting feelings overwhelmed her, and she suddenly couldn't read the words on the paper in her hands any longer. Jordan tugged her phone from her pocket and somehow managed to select Alex from her contact list. She wasn't surprised when it went to voicemail, and she left her friend a brief message informing her of the news.

Sammy responded obediently to her silent commands as she gestured to go out to the car. She couldn't bring herself to turn on the radio during the drive, and was mildly surprised when she made it to the lighthouse without any problems. She couldn't remember the last time she'd wept - truly *wept*. Her grief wasn't coming in the form of loud, cathartic sobs, or gasping hiccups. It had happened in the form of unrelenting silent tears, and nothing she thought or told herself stopped them.

The sea breeze felt soothing on her damp face. Samantha pressed herself up against Jordan's side as soon as she sat on the sand. Jordan leaned heavily against the dog, not bothering to try to hide her tears any longer. Her emotions ran the gambit; she teetered from grief to joy and back again, and she was suddenly too exhausted to try to make sense of them.

"Alex told me about your voicemail. I tried to call you," a tender voice called from the top of the dune. Jordan turned to see Chase approaching slowly, waiting for her to let him know that he could join her. Instead of responding, Jordan signaled with her head for him to come closer. Chase sat on the opposite side of her from Sammy, and immediately laced his fingers with hers. She stared down at their hands, and felt unbelievable peace knowing that they could finally hold hands without any fear of him facing consequences. They sat together in silence for a long time before Jordan finally realized she'd stopped crying and found her voice.

"I must have left my phone at home. I don't even remember putting it down after I called Alex." She rested her chin on his shoulder. "I spent so many years trying to do whatever it took to make Adam happy, I think the thought of finally being *actually free* of that pressure, that responsibility, was too much to process at first. It's not even that I feel guilty, because Alex helped me to get over that. I feel…" She sighed. "I feel sad that this is what it came to…that this is how my life turned out because I'd allowed myself to walk away from God for someone who wasn't worthy. But so much more than that; I'm excited for the journey that God has in store for my future." She looked up into Chase's warm brown eyes. A full, joyful smile spread across her face. "It's finally over."

Chase beamed back at her, and placed a tender kiss to her forehead. "Yeah, Jay…it is. It's finally over." He wiped the lingering tears from her cheeks with his thumbs, and she watched as his gaze flitted to her lips for the briefest instant. "You've got your whole life ahead of you now."

Jordan giggled and pulled away from him, offering a hand to encourage him to join her as she leapt to her feet. "And I'll be able to finish school without working thanks to the settlement from the hospital," she revealed. Chase pushed himself up as well, and used his grip on her hand to yank her against him. Jordan gave a soft 'oh!' of surprise as she braced herself against his chest, staring up at him with wide eyes. His own expression had become serious, and their breaths mingled when she unconsciously lifted herself onto her toes. She was sure that he was going to kiss her...

Until he suddenly pulled back and shattered the moment. "That's amazing," he breathed. Jordan couldn't decide if she was disappointed or relieved that he hadn't kissed her, and the look on his face suggested that he was experiencing the same warring feelings. Watching him try to compose himself led Jordan to settle on *relieved*. They would have their moment soon. But she didn't want it to be the very same *day* that she became legally divorced.

***

"Jordy, why did they kill me?"

"W-what?" Jordan looked around, confused by the sudden presence in her house. "Mi-Michael? Oh, Michael…I'm so sorry."

"Why couldn't you save me? You were supposed to help us!" He stalked towards her, brandishing a familiar pair of scissors.

"Michael, please put the scissors down. Let me help you."

"No! You're with the rogue police! You wanted me dead just like them!" He lunged for her, scissors aimed for her chest.

Jordan was wrenched from her nightmare with a heaving gasp. Each beat of her heart throbbed painfully in her chest, and her hand trembled when she reached over to turn on her lamp.

A cool, wet nose pressed into her shoulder, and Jordan rolled over to press her face into Sammy's side. The husky whined, her owner's sobs muffled in her thick fur. She curled around Jordan as much as she could.

"Why won't these dreams go *away*? I just want to forget it ever happened." She reached around Sammy to grab her phone, considering texting Alex or Chase. Maybe if she had a reminder that she wasn't *alone*, that they were getting through this mess *together*, she'd be able to get back to sleep. A glance at the time drew a grimace across her face. 4:25am. Three hours before they would be waking up. No way was she going to make either of them as tired as her just because she had a bad dream.

Jordan sighed, turned her lamp back off, and flopped onto her back. She stared at the ceiling for what felt like hours, too anxious to even close her eyes. If she fell asleep now, chances were high that she'd fall back into another nightmare. One visit from her deceased client was *plenty* for a single night.

Once light finally started to stream into her room, Jordan resigned herself to drag her sore, sluggish body out of bed. She stood under the shower in a daze, until the water ran cold. Her mind flitted from thought to thought restlessly, making it impossible for Jordan to focus or process anything. The disorganization in her mind left her feeling worn down and off-kilter. It was a shock that she'd even been able to get dressed and out the door, but before long she found herself in front of the one place that still felt safe: her church.

Jordan took a moment to collect herself. With significant effort, she pushed back the intrusive barrage of memories and plastered a smile on her face. Part of her was relieved that she wouldn't see Alex or Chase until after the service; they would be able to see right through her mask, and she *really* didn't want to fall apart in church. Afterwards, she could go to her spot and let it all out. Away from the prying eyes of her well-intentioned church family.

"God, give me strength to get through today," she breathed. One quick glance in her visor mirror, and she was out of her car. With each warm welcome and loving greeting, the smile on her face became less forced and more comfortable.

"Good morning, Jordan!" Mary, one of the other female vocalists on the worship team, greeted warmly. Jordan dropped her purse onto her chair and wrapped her arms around the other woman. "How are you feeling?"

"I'm alright," Jordan murmured into her shoulder, cherishing the embrace that reminded her so strongly of the hugs she desperately missed from her mother. "You give the *greatest* hugs, you know that?"

Mary chuckled and tightened her grip for a moment in response. "I've been told that before, yes."

Arms encircled Jordan from behind, and suddenly she was back in the hospital with scissors digging into her abdomen. Despite the way her lungs fought to drag in air, all of the oxygen had been abruptly sucked from the room. Voices echoed from all around her, but nothing sounded like English. She knew that if she couldn't breathe, she was going to pass out. If she passed out, they were going to kill Michael...and he was just spooked. He didn't *want* to hurt her.

"...get Alex. She....classroom. Jo...Jordan, can you...going on?"

The voice was familiar, but out of place. Mary didn't work at the hospital...

Oh. No. *Not* the hospital. Right...where? The iron grip on her lungs eased just enough to gasp in a breath or two, and Jordan blinked the darkness out of her eyes. Hands that she hadn't even felt released her. Without the support, Jordan stumbled forward into a strong, familiar pair of arms. *Chase.*

Reality crashed into her as her mind finally registered that she was safe...*not* back in the nightmare that had put her in the hospital weeks before. She buried her face into Chase's chest to muffle the sobs bubbling in her throat. Her feet followed blindly as he led her somewhere; the cool air that danced across the back of her neck gave her a hint as to where.

"I've got you, you're safe. It's just you and me, Jay. Let it out." His hand served as an anchor as it rubbed calming circles into her back, and his voice chased away the lingering ghosts. The steady thump of his heartbeat against her ear steadied her own pulse. "What's going on?" His cheek settled against the crown of her head, and Jordan took a slow, shuddering breath.

"I was standing and talking to Mary, then I was...back in the hospital, and I couldn't breathe. Someone must've hugged me from behind?" Questioning green eyes met Chase's worried gaze, and he nodded.

"I think it must've been Casey, she was pretty freaked when she came back looking for Alex," Chase murmured. He wiped the tears from her cheeks and tucked her hair behind her ear.

"Oh no...poor Casey, I need to talk to her. Tell her it's not her fault," Jordan whimpered. Chase held her shoulders firmly when she tried to turn back for the door.

"Alex is with her right now. Give yourself a minute to breathe. Has this happened before?" Chase questioned, voice gentle but serious.

Jordan shook her head. "No...this was the first time I've had a flashback. Dreams, I've had a few, but nothing while I was awake before now." She leaned against Chase again, grateful for his unwavering support as her exhaustion hit her hard.

"You've had dreams of what happened?" She nodded. Tears burned in her eyes again but she refused to let more fall.

"If you have another one and can't get back to sleep, I want you to call me, okay?"

"Chase..." She leaned back to look at him.

"I'm serious. You don't have to deal with this alone. If you want to move past this, to get past what just happened inside, you are going to have to face it head on, and you're nuts if you think I'm going to let you hide it from me."

This time, when tears tracked down her cheeks, he let them be. "Oh yeah, because *that's* so appealing: a girl who can't even be hugged without having a meltdown," she drawled, swiping at her face in frustration.

Chase surprised her by catching her wrists and wrapping his fingers around hers. His eyes were determined, and he waited for her to look at him before speaking. "Don't start pushing me away, Jordan. Don't shut me out now. You've been through hell, and if you don't deal with it you could wind up with PTSD. Cut yourself some slack, and lean on the people who love you. We aren't going to let you go. We are here every step of the way."

Jordan nodded, overwhelmed by his impassioned words. "Okay...okay. I think it's time to talk to someone about all of this, too. It's just getting worse." He nodded with a small, proud smile. Jordan heaved a sigh, finally allowing the tension to bleed from her shoulders. "Oh, man," she moaned abruptly. Her head dropped to his clavicle, and a questioning hum vibrated through his chest. "I just had a freakout in front of the entire church, and poor Casey doesn't have a clue what just happened."

"Well, on the bright side, it really wasn't the *entire* church. First service is always quieter," he pointed out lightly. "And Casey will be fine. Alex is going to bring her out here once we give her the okay. You ready for that?"

"Yeah, she needs to know it's not her fault." Chase let her go and ducked his head inside. A timid and tearful teen was followed out by a concerned best friend, who relaxed once she saw the look on Jordan's face. Chase remained beside Alex, who nudged Casey towards Jordan. "Oh, Case, come here sweetheart."

The raven-haired girl launched herself into Jordan's open arms with a sob. They held tightly to one another, and Jordan kissed her head. "I'm so sorry, JoJo. I didn't mean to upset you! I'm sorry!"

Jordan pulled back and bent to Casey's eye level. "You did nothing wrong, you understand me? I'm sorry you had to see that, but it was *not* your fault. I *love* your hugs, okay?" Casey nodded and clung to her once more. "I'm going to need a lot more of your hugs for a while, okay? What happened at work has me a bit out of sorts, but hugs *really* help me." She swayed back and forth slightly, humming to comfort Casey as she gradually relaxed.

"Casey, why don't you stay in the main sanctuary with JoJo when we go inside?" Alex offered gently. Once the teen nodded, she looked up to Chase. "You too. Brian already went back to cover your classroom." Chase squeezed her hand gratefully.

The four remained outside a few minutes longer, until Jordan was sure Casey was calm. She pressed an affectionate kiss to the girl's forehead and encouraged her to head in. Alex hugged her before following Casey into the church, and Jordan allowed Chase to lead her in with a warm, steady hand on the small of her back. The pastor raised a questioning brow at her, and gave a barely-perceptible nod when she gave him a thumbs-up. Chase led her to Casey, and settled into the seat to Jordan's left. She took a moment to watch him, by her side and unwavering in his support, and thanked God for the amazing support system He'd given her in Chase, Alex and Brian. As if he'd felt her eyes on him, Chase glanced at her, smiled tenderly, and laced his fingers through hers. Jordan stared at their joined hands for a long while, only half-listening to the words of her pastor.

"I think Alex wants to talk to you. Call me later, okay?" Chase's voice was low in her ear, and Jordan looked up at him to nod. He squeezed her hand and ducked out of the front door of the church. The brunette turned to see her best friend approaching.

"Walk and coffee?" Alex offered. In lieu of a response, she tucked her fingers around Alex's elbow and waved to Brian. "So, what happened earlier?"

"I had a...a flashback I guess. Casey hugged me from behind, and it must've triggered something. I've been out of it all morning; I had a nightmare last night and I couldn't fall back to sleep after."

Alex was silent for a long moment, but leaned against Jordan's arm as if to offer some strength. "How long have you been having the dreams?"

"Two weeks."

"The flashbacks?"

"That was the first. I think it's getting worse. H-have you had anything?" Alex nodded solemnly. "Lex...I think we need to talk to someone."

Alex nodded again. "Brian and I have talked about it. I've only had a few nightmares, but...well, you know how that messes with your day."

"Yeah...I can appreciate that."

"I don't want to bother Brian with it, you know? One of us needs to be on top of our game with the kids."

"You know I'm always here to talk, Lex...anytime."

"That goes both ways," Alex insisted. Tears filled her eyes suddenly, and Jordan tugged her to a stop. "I've never been so scared as I was that day. I felt like we'd stepped into another dimension, you know? No way could that have been real life. But then I heard the gunshot, I saw red...and then you fell." Jordan's heart broke as Alex gave in a shuddering sigh. "M-Matt was the one who pulled you away from Michael and said that you were breathing. I...I think he could see my shock. He called for me to help him, told me what do until the EMT's got there. That helped to ground me...feeling your heartbeat while I tried to stop the bleeding. I'm pretty sure that's what kept me from having a breakdown right then and there."

Jordan pulled her best friend into a tight hug. "I'm sorry you had to go through that, Lex. I'm sorry we haven't talked about this before now. What do you think about going to see a counselor together, at least for a little while? I think having you there might help me sort through everything."

Alex gave a teary nod and then tugged her to continue walking. "Okay. We can figure that out later. Now. How's it feel to finally be a single woman again?"

Jordan gave a soft laugh. "I honestly haven't had the energy to think much about it. I mean...when I told Chase about the papers we almost kissed, but-"

"Wait, *almost*?!"

"Yes, *almost*. I'm glad he didn't do it, to be honest. It would've been, I dunno, *wrong* somehow if we got together immediately after the divorce was finalized. I think it needs to wait until I've got this worked out, you know? He's been an amazing friend. Like today...I *need* that from him right now."

The pair paused their conversation when they reached the coffee shop and placed their orders. As they began the brief walk back to the church, they continued chatting, and Jordan thanked God for the beautiful, strong woman beside her, and the unconditional love and support they'd shared for years.

Epilogue - October

"How have your dreams been this week?"

A genuine smile spread across Jordan's face as she thought back on her sleep since the last time she saw her therapist. "Better. Much better...it took a little while to get to sleep a few nights, but no nightmares."

"That's wonderful to hear, Jordan. It's not going to be better overnight, and you may have more nightmares still, but progress is progress."

She nodded eagerly, and settled back into the soft chair. "It's been getting better since I started opening up about everything to Alex and Chase. I think it's been helping Alex too; she seems to be a little more relaxed in general, and told me that she's been handling it all better too. I hate that what happened put her through so much."

"Well, consider it from her perspective. As traumatic as the event was for you to experience first hand, she watched someone that she loves go through it without being able to do anything. That is traumatic in its own right."

"Yeah...I couldn't imagine if the roles were reversed."

Silence settled over the pair for a few moments, and for the first time since she started seeing her therapist, Jordan realized it was comfortable. "Tell me more about Chase."

She couldn't help the tug of her lips thinking about him. "He's been wonderful through all of this, so patient and understanding. It's been hard to take it slow, to keep it...*platonic* until I've got things worked out."

"That's important to you."

"Yeah. It wouldn't be fair to him to jump in before I have my anxiety under control. He's been beside me all through this, listening and being that shoulder to cry on when I don't want to bother Alex any more. He deserves to be with someone who is ready to give him just as much support; right now all I am able to do is *take* his support. I don't want that to be where we begin."

"You've already come a long way from where you started, Jordan. If he has been the one that you've turned to when you have needed the support of someone you care about, if he has been your rock, what would you say is separating where you are now from when you are in a relationship with him?"

Jordan sat back for a moment and thought about what she'd just been asked. "I...I don't know. When I first started coming here, I was having breakdowns and flashbacks in the middle of the day. I couldn't stand the thought of him having to deal with that while we were on a date or something...but I guess you make a really good point. I was waiting to be more stable before I allowed myself to really let him in, and I'm pretty much there. It's always going to be a problem to work through, but..." She trailed off as she pondered her next words. "But there's no more reason to keep him at arm's length."

Her therapist smiled warmly, and nodded. "It sounds like you need to have a conversation with Chase."

"Yeah. It doesn't really make sense to drag this out any more. I have nothing to be afraid of with him; I *know* he has my best interest at heart. I know he understands everything that has happened, he's lived the last year-and-change *with* me. I'm not going to let my anxiety get in the way anymore."

The smile morphed into a knowing look. "Good. See you same time next week?" Jordan nodded with a grin. "Good luck, Jordan, I can't wait to hear how things go."

"Thanks, you've been a Godsend. See you next week!" With that, Jordan hurried out the door. Before she got to her car, she tugged her phone from her purse. 'Hey, are you busy?'

Chase's response was relatively quick. 'Not at all, what's up?'

'Meet me at the lighthouse in 15?'

'Be right there.'

When Jordan pulled up to her favorite spot, Sammy in tow, she couldn't contain her grin at the sight of Chase leaning casually against his car. The affection in his gaze as she approached stole her breath away, and she wrapped her arms around his waist. His chuckle reverberated through her chest when she tried to burrow closer for protection from the chilly October air.

"Hello to you too, sunshine. Good session today?"

Jordan tipped her head back, and stared into sparkling brown eyes. "Something like that." He gave her no resistance when she laced their fingers and tugged him along the beach. "Megan helped me to realize something today."

Chase watched her silently, kicking his shoes off above the line left by the waves. She followed suit, and both were momentarily distracted by Sammy's bounding charge into the breaking ocean. Foam tickled her toes, and Jordan was reminded of a time not so long ago, when Chase had first run into her in that same spot. "So what was this epiphany of yours?"

Warm eyes held her own when she turned to face him, and butterflies started to stir in her stomach. Jordan took a steadying breath, and grinned when concern started to seep into his expression. "I've been keeping you at arm's length for months, for a few different reasons. But it all boils down to fear; I was afraid to let you in completely; afraid to give you the power to hurt me like Adam did, afraid to admit that you *wouldn't* hurt me like Adam did. Afraid that I would never be able to give to you a *fraction* of what you've given to me through all of this. It didn't feel...*fair* to you, welcoming you into the mess that is my life."

The bemused look on his face spoke volumes. "If you wanted to keep me out of your mess, you failed miserably. We both know there wasn't much of a chance of that."

Jordan nodded, dropping her gaze to the sand. "You're right, and I'm sorry for letting all of that get in the way. I'm sorry that it took me this long to reach this point."

Calloused fingers cradled Jordan's jaw and drew her eyes back up to meet his. "I don't want you to ever apologize again for taking the time that you needed to work through everything. I told you I wasn't going to leave you to do it alone, and I meant it. I won't take a step until you're ready."

"I don't deserve you," Jordan whispered, tears sliding down her cheeks.

"You deserve to be *loved*, Jordan. You deserve to be *respected* and *cherished*. It may take a while for you to believe that, but I'll make sure it sinks in."

She curled her fingers around his hands, reassuring herself that his touch was real. "I'm afraid I'll lose myself like I did before..."

"You've come too far to forget who you are. You are surrounded by people who will hold you accountable to God and to yourself every day. *I* won't let that happen. Your passion for God is part of what I love about you, and part of my duty to you is to make sure you don't let that go. Baby steps though, Jay. Doing this right means taking our time."

Silently, the brunette sent up a prayer of gratitude for the incredible gift that was the man before her. She felt confident, calm for the first time in months, that everything was *right*. With a grin, she rocked herself forward onto her toes and pressed her lips to his. Chase responded immediately, dropping one hand to press against the small of her back and draw her closer. Outside noise fell away, and she hummed in contentment. He traced her bottom lip with his tongue, but as she started to react, he pulled away.

"Oh man," he breathed.

"*Finally.*"

His rich, whole-hearted laughter was *definitely* one of her all-time favorite sounds; that was *almost* enough to make her pause and soak it in, but the need to kiss him again won out.

***

Holding true to his word, Chase gave her complete control. In the week since she'd kissed him, Jordan had been the one to initiate every display of affection. With anyone else it would have given her all kinds of insecurities, but she'd caught the twitch in his fingers when he had to hold himself back from grabbing her hand, and the way he would stare at her mouth until she leaned in. As grateful as she was for his restraint, they'd kept their feelings in check long enough. It had been near impossible to sit still through the sermon, and Chase had picked up on her energy immediately. The moment the final song ended, he turned to her expectantly.

"Okay, what is *wrong* with you today?"

"I want you to take me out for lunch," she stated matter of factly. Chase raised an amused eyebrow at her, but she could read the spark of excitement in his eyes. Alex, who'd been approaching the pair from behind Chase, might as well have been a cartoon character with the surprised look on her face and the way she spun on her heel and made a beeline back to her husband.

"You do, do you?" Chase drawled with an easy smile on his face. "And what would be the occasion for taking a lovely Jaybird such as yourself out to lunch on this fine day?"

Jordan leaned forward into his personal space, stopping inches away. Chase tilted his chin up as if daring her to kiss him in the middle of the still-half-full church. She steeled her resolve but didn't move back, grinning. "I've spent too long learning what the wrong kind of relationship looks like, forcing my own agenda. I'm done standing in the way of God's plan. I'm ready to be shown what it looks like to be *respected and cherished*. What are you waiting for, Falkland?"

Affection sparkled in his brown eyes and he tugged her into the aisle "Nothing anymore, *Evans*." Alex squeezed Jordan's free hand excitedly as they passed their friends, and she found it impossible to stop beaming like a complete goofball.

With the love of her true friends, the love of a good man, and the love of God, Jordan felt full and bright as she followed the path unfolding before her.

Acknowledgements

This book has always been one that was more therapeutic than planned for publishing. It has been a process of understanding who I was in the darkest time of my life, and shifting the narrative to become something that I used rather than something that hurt me. That being said, this book would not have existed if not for the difficult experiences that drew me closer to God than I'd ever been, and shaped me into a stronger individual.

Above all else, I give thanks to my complex, loving, just God. I never thought I'd be able to express gratitude for trials, but it is in those times I have been able to see Him most clearly, and it is in those times that I am best able to understand that He never abandons us. I thank Him for creative expression, for opportunities to use that creative expression to hopefully help others feel seen and heard.